To Jewel
Hope you enjoy the
story.
Deborah D. Hagy
Debbie
6-8-2019

THE
PERFECT
PICTURE

DEBERA HAGY

WESTBOW·
PRESS
A DIVISION OF THOMAS NELSON
& ZONDERVAN

WestBow Press books may be ordered through booksellers or by contacting:

WestBow Press
A Division of Thomas Nelson & Zondervan
1663 Liberty Drive
Bloomington, IN 47403
www.westbowpress.com
1 (866) 928-1240

ISBN: 978-1-4908-9918-3 (sc)
ISBN: 978-1-4908-9923-7 (hc)
ISBN: 978-1-4908-9921-3 (e)

Library of Congress Control Number: 2015911300

Print information available on the last page.

WestBow Press rev. date: 07/14/2015

To Jan, the best kind of friend anyone could ever ask for. Thank you so very much for believing in me and encouraging me as I wrote this book. I don't know what I would do without our special friendship. We've shared so many special moments when we laughed and cried and shared heartfelt feelings that we wouldn't dare to share with anyone else. You've always kept me accountable for my actions and have helped me through a lot of difficult times. Thank you for your prayers, your friendship, and your love.

To my daughter, Mikki, whom I love so deeply. Thank you for taking time out of your busy life to read my manuscripts and give me your honest opinion. I'm so proud of the strong Christian woman you've become. I watch as you constantly give yourself to your family, friends and church. The eight children you have raised show how much you care and devote yourself to others. You did a great job with them. I will always be just a phone call away and will be by your side whenever you need me.

CHAPTER 1

Deidre Hugely and her two teenage granddaughters, Carissa and André, didn't know what to expect as they walked into the law office of Talbot and Talbot. They were confused and had mixed feelings about the whole situation. They had just lost a very special person in their lives—a situation that had led them to this law office—so they were anxious to find out what all this was about and what it had to do with them. An assistant of a lawyer had called Deidre a week earlier and asked if she and her two granddaughters could meet in the law office of Talbot and Talbot for the reading of their deceased friend's will.

Feeling shock and confusion, Deidre had told the assistant, "I'm not sure what this has to do with us, but I'll contact my granddaughters and see what their schedules are and if they can come."

The assistant had explained that attorneys could not conduct the reading of the will unless all three of them were present. Deidre made arrangements with the girls and called the assistant back and agreed to meet as requested.

Deidre's granddaughters had dozens of questions, but Deidre couldn't answer any of them.

"I don't know any more than you do. We're just going to have to wait and see when we get there." That didn't stop the questions, and then the girls' imaginations started getting the best of them.

"Maybe he was a millionaire, and he's giving all his money to us," Carissa said. But André had a bigger imagination than Carissa.

"Maybe he was a king of some country and was in hiding, and now we are going to be princesses. And Grandma, you'll be the queen." Deidre didn't say a word. She understood their imaginations because she was known for her unique imagination.

In a more serious tone, André added, "Maybe it's just a last good-bye or something like that."

The law office wasn't large or elegant, but it wasn't a tacky, low-budget office either. The waiting room was a warm color with a deep wooden wainscot that went all around the room but only as high up the wall as the back of the chairs in the room. The chairs were tan, made of cloth, and had dark brown legs. There were three end tables and one coffee table that had been made from a dark wood. The three large pictures in the room were scenic oil paintings. There was a television hanging in the corner, but it wasn't on at the time. There was a door that had a note on it saying to enter, so Deidra told the girls to wait there as she went to find out where they were to go and what to do.

The receptionist greeted Deidra by her name, smiling and extending her hand.

"Hello, Deidra. My name is June. I'm Mark Talbot's assistant. I hope you didn't have any trouble finding us. Are Carissa and André with you?" Deidra nodded.

"Yes, they're waiting in the other room, and they're about to bust open with curiosity." June just smiled. She looked to be in her early fifties and was dressed very professionally. She wore her hair short, and her nails showed evidence of a professional manicure. She was as tall as Deidra and wore glasses. After introductions June had them follow her. She made them feel a little more at ease as she escorted them to the office where they were to meet with others so that they could read the will that their friend had left. Just before she entered the room, Deidra stopped to look behind her to see if the girls were close. She paused just in time to have them both run into her, which made all three of them snicker. As they entered the room, Mark Talbot stepped up to them, his hand out to introduce himself. Deidre was surprised by how young he was.

"Hi, I'm Mark Talbot, Edward Talbot's son. After my father's death, I took over the law firm and all of my father's clients. I'm glad you could come. Please have a seat, and we'll all get acquainted."

Just then Deidra noticed the others in the very large room. She knew a few of them. They were her friends—and friends of her deceased friend—and she recognized others who had attended the funeral. Two others, accompanied by their spouses, were the children of her friend. She knew from her deceased friend that they were just a few years younger than her. The woman was very thin, and she had dried, bleached-blond hair. Her skin was so pale, but her eyes were the brightest blue that she had ever seen. Her brother was thin but looked healthy. He had blondish gray hair, which, Deidre thought, was probably the real color of the woman's hair. He had a nice tan, and his eyes were the same color as his sister's.

The attorney proceeded to introduce everyone. He had barely finished the introductions when the daughter abruptly spoke up. "I don't mean to be rude, but I don't understand why these strangers are here. What do they have to do with my father's will? I mean, surely nothing of any value would have been left to them. I saw all of you at the funeral. We know why the others were there, but what do you have to do with our father?"

Deidre, the girls, and a few other members of Deidre's family had attended the funeral, but they'd stayed in the background and didn't try to interfere with anything or anyone. Deidre and the girls along with some friends were the ones who had made all the arrangements. Everything was planned and paid for in advance. All they had to do was take the clothes to the funeral home and place the ad in the paper. They'd contacted the few friends he had, and they'd ordered the flowers. They'd had Mark, the lawyer, call the children. Deidra was about to answer the daughter when Mark interrupted, "All of this will be explained today. Your father has left a letter and a video explaining everything. Now may we get started? There's a lot to go over, and it will take some time to get through everything."

Deidra was growing more confused as the conversation went on, but she just sat in her chair, waiting to hear what was next.

Deidra was checking out the room where they had gathered. She came to the conclusion that it must have been a conference room of some sort. Once again, the decor of the room featured soft colors with dark wood on some of the walls. Mark continued to explain the format of the meeting and what was going to transpire during the meeting. "First there is a letter to be read and then a video to watch, and then after that, there will be the reading of the will. I believe you're the one, who helped with the letter and the video, aren't you, André?" Deidre quickly looked over at her granddaughter in complete surprise.

André shyly nodded her head. Okay, now Deidre was really confused. André looked at her grandmother and whispered, "You'll understand in a minute."

Their deceased friend's daughter was really upset now and once again interrupted the meeting to make sure she had spoken her mind clearly. "I don't like the sound of any of this. What did you talk my father into doing? How could you take advantage of a poor old man like that?"

André, not sounding a bit shy this time, spoke up firmly and with a little agitation, "I didn't make him do anything. He asked for my help, and I did everything he wanted. That's all."

Once again Mark stepped in to explain things so they could continue. "Please … I promise that you will understand everything, if you just wait and listen to the letter and video." Once again everyone became silent and was ready to listen to the last words of Ben Crawford, Deidre's friend, written and recorded for everyone to hear.

Mark began reading. "Dear Cassie and Casey, you have just met part of my adopted family—Deidre, Carissa, and André." Ben's daughter, Cassie, made a groaning noise and was about to say something when Mark put this finger to his lips, indicating not to interrupt. Ben's son, Casey, who was sitting next to Cassie, placed his hand on her hand.

"And Deidre, Carissa, and André, you have just met my twin children, Cassie and Casey, and hopefully my son and daughter in-law. And then there are my dear friends—John, Sara, and their son, Daniel—who were always there for me. I'm not sure if any of you met at my funeral, but today you will get to know each other a lot more. My sweet André is helping me to write this letter, and André, they won't think you said that."

That made Deidre, the girls, and the few friends chuckle, but the others did not. Deidra noticed that Casey did smile. But Cassie's lips were tight, and her face was stern and angry.

When he turned his eyes back to the text of the will, Mark continued, "Cassie and Casey, I want to tell you all about Deidre and her family, how I met all of them, and what an impact they had on my life. At a time when I was just sitting and waiting to die and join your sweet mother, they brought me back to life. Because of them, the last year has been a beautiful experience. I was going to have André write all this down, but then she suggested and explained to me that we could make a video of it. That way there would be no misunderstanding. She feels that everyone would love to see me talk about all this just as if I were there with all of you."

Deidre looked over at André. She already had tears in her eyes as she looked at her grandmother with a tender and sweet smile. Deidre was so proud of her. She had loved Ben so much and was always ready to do anything for him.

Speaking Ben's written words, Mark read, "So I guess it's time to start up this movie. I feel like some kind of movie star doing this. André assures me it will be fun, but that camera in my face makes me a little nervous."

Mark then closed the letter and reached for his remote control to start the video. Before he could start the video, Cassie started complaining again. "How long is this video? Should I go to the restroom and get some water, and is there popcorn with this movie?" She went too far this time, and it was Casey that spoke up this time.

"Cassie, what is wrong with you? This is going to be our father talking on this video. Why are you making things so difficult? Just sit there and be quiet so the rest of us can listen to what Dad wants to say to us."

Cassie wasn't about to let that happen. "When did you start wanting to hear what dear old Dad has to say? Have you forgotten the reason we both got out of that rat hole. He was all talk and never had any desire to improve our lifestyle. Our poor mother had to live in his meager, nonexistent world."

Mark tried to intervene so that they could continue with everything that had to be covered, but he was not successful.

"This has nothing to do with the past or what happened between any of us. It's about closure. I myself would like to get all this over with and get back to my life with what is entitled to me. I think you feel the same way, so please no more interruption, and let's get our inheritance and go home."

That seemed to quiet Cassie, but Deidre was steaming inside. She looked over at her girls, and they showed concern on their faces. Carissa was concerned about the look on her grandmother's face, so she leaned over to whisper to her. "It'll all be okay, Grandma. Just remember how happy Ben was with us and how much we loved each other." Her grandmother didn't lose her temper very often, but when she did, it was always something no one wanted to experience. So she knew she had to calm her down before she tore into both of Ben's children.

Finally Mark was able to start the video. Seeing Ben on the screen instantly brought tears to Deidre's eyes. She looked over at her granddaughters and saw their tears. Carissa was also busy looking over at Daniel, John, and Sara's son. They were both the same age and had become very fond of each other. The only ones who had no reaction were Ben's children and their spouses.

There was Ben with that loving smile and that twinkle in his eye. Oh, how she missed him.

"Are we on?" You could hear André in the background assuring him that the camera was going.

"Wow, it's hard to know where to start. I guess I'll start with how I felt on the day my three angels entered my life. I call them my angels because I know it was God that sent them to me. I was tired of waiting to die and was thinking about maybe hurrying the process up."

Deidre was shocked when she heard what he had just said because she had never known or heard him say anything indicating he felt that way. She looked at André since she must have known. After all, she was the one recording this. André just gave half of an "I'm sorry" smile at her grandmother.

"And the next thing I knew these angel's came rushing into my life and changed everything. I was no longer lonely or bored. They kept me on my toes, and I sure learned a lot from them."

Deidre and the family couldn't believe how he had died so quickly. He started feeling tired and then weak. They had just learned that he had cancer, and then a few weeks later he came down with pneumonia. He quickly went downhill from there. It was like he had reached a certain point of happiness and then felt it was time to go home to his Lord and his wife.

Ben talked about his wife, Annie, a lot. From what they had heard from Ben, the two of them loved each other very much. Even though Deidre and girls never met Annie, she sounded like a good godly woman. In a way, if it hadn't been for Annie, they might not have met Ben.

As Ben continued with his story, Deidre got lost in her own thoughts about how they had met Ben. It may have been more than a year ago, but it just seemed like a month ago. It all happened in such a strange way. Deidre felt the same way that Ben felt. It was meant to be, and God had directed them to him because Ben needed them and they needed him.

CHAPTER 2

Deidre was a professional event photographer. She loved photography, but she never got the chance to do the kind of photography that she dreamed of. She wanted to work for a magazine and travel to different countries and see different cultures. But she fell in love and ended up having a family at a young age. But once the children grew up, she went back to school and received her degree in photography and then started her own photography business called Special Moments. She takes photos of births, birthdays, weddings, anniversaries, baptisms, etc. She was good at her work and had become very well known. She would travel to all parts of Indiana. Many times when she was traveling to a location, she would spot something and have to stop to take a picture of it. Both of her granddaughters loved photography but didn't quite have the passion for it like Deidre did. There were times when Deidre would see some great locations for photos and would take Carissa or André or both back with her to get some shots.

Carissa and André were both in college. Carissa was in her second year, and André was in her first. All their lives they were close cousins. They were alike in a lot of ways yet also very different. They were both medium in height and medium in build like their grandmother. Carissa had blond hair and blue eyes. André had dark brown hair and green eyes like her grandmother. They had a lot in common too. They both loved photography, and they both adored their grandmother. Carissa was an art student at IUPUI in Indianapolis, and she was taking a summer course to explore photography. André always loved photography but wasn't sure what she wanted to pursue at college. She had a couple of interests, so she was taking some basic classes at Ivy Tech.

Deidre had an eye for color, light, and uniqueness, so Carissa asked her grandma to take her for a drive and help her find things to photograph.

In the fall her class was going to have a showing, and there would be awards handed out in different divisions. She knew she would have to compete against fourth-year art students, but she felt between her and her grandmother, they could give them a run for their money.

Deidra was so happy Carissa asked for her help, and of course, she gladly said yes. They made arrangements to take a whole day driving and looking. Naturally Carissa invited André to come along because it just wouldn't be as exciting without her. Deidre informed them, "You'll have to get up early because it will take some time and effort to find just the right subjects and lighting to photograph."

On that Saturday the girls spent the night at their grandparent's house so that they knew they would be up on time. Deidre always woke up early, and this morning as she was sitting on her back deck and drinking her coffee, she thought about the day and looked forward to being with her girls. It felt good to be needed, and she was excited about the day ahead. There was a little fog that morning, but she felt it would burn off early.

Brad, her husband, came out with his coffee and joined her on the patio. He knew how much she loved her granddaughters, and he also knew that she was really looking forward to the day.

"So do you think the girls will be able to keep up with you?"

Deidre just snickered. "You mean me keeping up with them? I'm the one who is sixty-one years old." She didn't look or act her age. She kept herself healthy and in good shape. They both did. But she did have to admit that she was slowing down a little.

"I think you'll keep them on their toes. Do you know which direction you're going to go?" Last night she had told Brad she wasn't sure if they would drive east or south. She would just have to sleep on it.

"I've decided to drive east toward the morning sun on I-70 a ways and then get off halfway from here to Richmond. There are some small older towns around there, and I think there might be some old and unique things that might be interesting."

"Just be careful on those back roads and stay safe." Brad was always so protective of her and sometimes a little overprotective. But after forty years of marriage, she was used to it. Plus Brad knew he had to let her be her own self.

They dated shortly after high school and were married when she was twenty-one years old. Deidre was always so proud of her husband, and she always thought he was a good-looking man. Brad worked and went to school at night to become an ophthalmologist. Deidre did some photography on the side and did some babysitting to make extra money. They had three children and seven grandchildren. The family was very close and meant the world to them, even though one daughter had moved out of town with her husband and two children, which meant they didn't get to see them very often.

Brad and Deidre were startled when the two girls came walking out to the patio, dressed and ready to go.

"Let's go, Grandma. Time and lighting is wasting away." Carissa was a lot more awake than André. Brad and Deidre looked at each other and just laughed.

Brad kissed each of the girls' cheeks. "You take it easy on poor old grandma, okay?"

"Yeah, right. I think it might be the other way around." André knew her grandmother's energy level. Her grandmother invented the phrase "Shop till you drop."

Naturally the girls needed to stop at McDonalds to get a breakfast sandwich. Deidre had packed some food and a cooler for later because she didn't know if they would be near any places where they could eat once they got on the back roads, and she didn't what to get caught out in the middle of nowhere with two hungry teenagers.

The fog wasn't burning off as fast as Deidre would have liked. They had been driving for about twenty minutes, and Deidre saw something that might be interesting, so she pulled the car over to the emergency lane. The sun was shining through a group of trees, and the fog enhanced the look. They all three got out, and she reminded Carissa of what she taught her about light and angles. They took a few pictures and then went back to the car, and they were off once again. The next stop was about ten miles down the road where they saw an old sign. Only a portion of it still showed, and next to it was an old windmill. This time André suggested to Carissa what angle to go with. But Carissa knew how close and what color contrast to use.

Next stop was five miles down, and this time it got a little tricky. Carissa wanted to take a picture of a cemetery that was off in the distance, and there was a large old tree by it. She wanted to shoot it in black and white, which Deidre thought was a great idea. The only problem was they couldn't get the angle right. So she climbed on a railing while her grandmother held on to her legs. Carissa wobbled back and forth until she finally got her balance. André started yelling and laughing at the same time. "You guys are nuts. You're going to kill yourself, and I'll have to drive Grandma's car home all by myself." Both girls loved driving their grandmother's car. It was little and sporty. As Carissa was taking the picture of the cemetery, André was taking a picture of Carissa on the rail with her grandmother holding on to her.

After that bright idea, Deidre decided it was time to take the exit off the interstate. She had seen it before and wanted to go back some time to explore what she had seen at a glance. There was an old church that had been abandoned years ago. Everything around it was overgrown to the point you could barely see the church. She never really told the girls what she had planned, and they didn't seem to mind. Carissa was busy looking at the pictures she had taken.

"Oh, Grandma, some of these are so cool," Carissa said. "I bet the professor will pick something out of these that he likes, and I'll get to put them in the showing."

Shortly after they took the exit, André saw the church. "Oh, Grandma, are we going over there to that old church?" You could hear the excitement in her voice.

At that time Carissa looked up from her camera and saw the church. "Wow, did you know this was here, Grandma?"

"I saw a glance of it from the interstate a few times and wanted to come back and explore it someday, so I thought all three of us could explore it today." Deidre couldn't wait to go see it and was glad the girls sounded just as excited about it as she was.

There was a lot of tall brush, some small trees, and very tall grass all around the church. The church was small and had brick all the way around. There were three long, narrow window frames on each side of the church that were curved on the top. There were no windows any longer. There was a brick chimney on the back side, and it was all there. There was a door frame that was curved on top but no door, and there were two small windows on each side that were placed close to the top of the door. Once again there were no actual windows.

The three of them worked their way into the church. It was a single-room church with just one small room right off from the door. Parts of the roof were missing. There wasn't a single thing left inside, not any wood from the pews or from an altar or any glass from the windows, which meant the congregation had probably taken these with them. Inside there was only weeds and brush.

"It's a church that died," Carissa commented. She spoke softly as not to disturb anyone.

Speaking just as softly, André said, "Maybe they built a bigger and better church, and no one wanted their old church."

Deidre felt such a peace and serenity there. "I bet there are a lot of stories to be told of the things that happened here long ago. Let's get some pictures and move on." They all three got some great shots of the light shining through the open windows and holes in the roof. They took numerous pictures of the outside with everything grown around it and the chimney with bricks that were missing here and there. Then it was time to move on.

Deidre continued down the road for just a short time. It was and old two-lane road.

André was in the backseat and was quiet for some time. Then she started looking around. "Hey, Grandma, do you know where you're going? We're not going to get lost, are we?"

Deidre smiled as she looked in the rearview mirror. "I'll know where I'm going when I get there. And if we do get lost, it won't be for long." She thought André would think that was funny, but she didn't even smile. She just kept looking out the window.

Deidre stopped rather suddenly. Both girls looked at her and at what they thought she might be looking at. André didn't like what she thought her grandmother might be thinking.

"What are you looking at, Grandma? That's just some old road that's overgrown. Besides there's an old mailbox with half of a name on it, which means its private property." Deidra didn't say anything at first. She got out of the car and took a couple of pictures of the mailbox with the road next to it. She got back into the car and backed it up and started down the old road. André didn't like this one bit.

"Grandma, what are you doing? This scares me. What if someone shoots us for being on their property or kidnaps us?"

Deidra had no idea why she wanted to go down this road, but she knew for some strange reason, they would be safe. "Trust me, hon. I know we'll be all right. I wouldn't do anything that I thought would bring you any harm. Just think of it as an adventure."

André softly said under her breath, "I don't like adventures."

The road was narrow and very rough. There were tree branches and rocks covering the road, some of them rather large. There wasn't a lot of sunlight because of the amount of trees, and everything was overgrown.

Carissa was more concerned about how nervous André was than their whereabouts. She was curious about what they may find. "Grandma, maybe we should think about leaving. It's really not right to be on someone's property that we don't know."

Deidre knew Carissa was right, but something was driving her to go on. "Just a little farther until I can find an area wide enough to turn around."

Right at that moment, Deidre spotted something. She stopped the car and stared for a moment. Then she opened the door slowly. "Let's go take a look over there where the sun is beaming through the trees. I think I see something."

André couldn't believe what she was hearing, let alone what she was seeing. Carissa was getting out too. "Are you guys nuts? We can't just start roaming around on someone's property. This is crazy. I'm staying in the car."

But when she saw they were going without her, she decided she didn't want to stay in the car alone, so she got out and started catching up with them. "You guys weren't really going to leave me in the car by myself, were you? Wait for me. Come on, guys. I'm a little scared."

At that moment she tripped over a large limb and fell in a pile of leaves. Both Deidre and Carissa came running to her. When they helped her up, they could see how upset she was, so Deidre hugged her tightly. "You're okay, sweetheart."

André wasn't crying, but she was really shaken up. "I don't like it here. Can we go back to the car? We're supposed to be taking pictures, not trespassing on somebody's scary property."

Deidre took her hand and gently started leading her. "I think there is something here. Don't ask me why, but I really feel we need to be here. And I sense that we are totally safe. Let's just go a little farther where the sun is shining through the trees."

The walk got a little more difficult. They had to climb over downed trees and move hanging branches out of the way. There were large rocks and holes they had to watch out for, and then there they were.

Rays of sunlight was streaming through the trees and shining on a grave. There was still a little fog mixed in with the sunlight. The three of them stood there, just looking at the gravestone. There was something so radiate about the way the light was shining on it. It hadn't been kept up. There were tree limbs and lots of leaves all over it.

Carissa broke the silence that was over them. "There's something so peaceful and angelic about it, but it's so sad too. I think I'll clear some of the debris away and take some shots."

"No, you should take a shot the way it is first and then maybe clear some stuff away."

André was getting better at seeing things and putting feeling into pictures.

Deidre agreed, and between the three of them taking pictures, there wasn't an angle that was missed. They could barely see the writing on the stone because of a large tree limb that blocked the stone. It took both Deidre and Carissa to move it, and André cleared away the smaller limbs. Then they stopped to see who the grave belonged to. It said, "The Love of My Life, My Annie.

Then there was the date of birth and death.

"There's no last name." Carissa was whispering in respect of the deceased.

"There doesn't need to be. She lived here in the woods somewhere." André wasn't whispering, but she spoke softly.

"Well, since we're visiting, let's clean things up a little around here, and then Carissa, you can take some more pictures." For some reason Deidre was starting to feel a little anxious.

They cleaned up the grave site and all around it. Then Carissa continued to take more pictures. Deidre was suggesting certain angles because of the lighting. She didn't notice that André had roamed off.

André wasn't the inquisitive type, but she felt compelled to look around a little. She no longer was nervous or frightened. She found a group of flowers growing in another spot where the sun found room to shine through the trees. She took some pictures and then thought it would be nice to pick them and put them on Annie's grave. When she started back, she realized she wasn't quite sure where to go. She must have gone farther than she had thought. For a quick moment, she panicked, but it passed quickly when something farther in the woods caught her eye. It was shiny. It looked like the sun was shining on something metal. She slowly started walking through the woods toward it.

Deidre stepped back to watch Carissa as she figured out different angles on her own. She turned to see if André was taking pictures of anything, and she realized she was nowhere in sight. At first she wasn't too concerned because André didn't like this place, so she doubted her daughter was very far.

When Carissa was finished, she called out, "Come on, André. We're done here, so let's head out."

Nothing!

Deidre yelled louder, "André, answer me! Where are you? It's time to go."

Carissa heard André's voice faintly. "Grandma, I heard her from over there. But she sounds so far away, and I couldn't understand what she said." She was pointing deeper into the woods.

They both started in the direction that Carissa heard André. They continued yelling for her, and both of them heard her this time.

"You're getting closer, but I can't tell you where I am. Keep coming this way. You'll see a shiny item in the woods soon. Just follow it." André's voice didn't sound frightened, so that made Deidre a little less frantic. They yelled a couple more times and continued to follow André's voice.

Finally they could see her through the trees, and they also could see the shiny item she was talking about. When they reached her, they realized that they were at a barn of some kind and that the shiny object was a piece of sheet metal. Deidre grabbed André and held her so tight that André had to ask her to let up.

"I was so scared. Why in the world would you take off like that? You'd think you were some little kid I had to make hold my hand so you won't run off. This is the woods. Anything could have happened. What were you thinking?"

André waited until her grandmother calmed down before she even tried to talk to her. "You said you felt it was safe here, and you know what? I feel the same way. I agree with you that there's a reason we're here. Let's go check this place out."

Now it was Deidre's turn to remind them that this was private property. "I don't think that's very wise. I think it's time to go back to the car.

Carissa agreed with her grandmother. "I think Grandma's right. Besides, I'm hungry so let's start heading back."

As they were starting to turn back, they all three stopped when they heard someone's voice calling out.

CHAPTER 3

Deidre's thoughts were interrupted by Ben's voice on the tape telling his version of the first time he met her and the girls.

"The morning was foggy, and I didn't want to even try to walk or do anything. I just didn't have the energy, strength, or desire. It had been weeks since I had even stepped off the porch. Walking through the house was a chore in itself. I no longer walked. I scooted, and even then to get from one room to the other, I would have to hold on to something and then sit down every chance I had. I was tired and lonely, and I just didn't care any longer. I just wanted to be with Annie and away from here."

It didn't take much for Cassie to chime in and say, "You have got to be kidding! Did I just hear what I thought I heard? Did he say he wanted to be away from there, the one place he demanded to stay no matter the cost, which was losing his own children and the death of his wife?"

Mark had turned off the video while Cassie ranted on, "This is nothing but a pack of lies. Why do we have to sit here and listen to all his manipulating lies?"

Casey stopped Cassie before she could say anything else. "Cassie, don't you understand you have to listen to the video if you want your share of the inheritances. Besides, I think I want to hear more about what it was like for him and his feelings."

Cassie glared at her brother with disgust in her eyes. "Are you joking? You aren't honestly falling for all this, are you? It's just his last chance to put a guilt treatment on us."

Casey once again placed his hand on his sister's hand. "I want to listen to what he has to say, and I want you to please sit there so that we can get this over with. I really don't want to be here any longer than I have to, and you're making it a lot longer."

That seemed to satisfy Casey, but Deidre was really struggling with her emotions. It was clear where Cassie stood when it came to her father, but she couldn't quite grasp how Casey felt. One moment he acted like he wanted to hear and know what his father had to say, and then the next moment he was acting like he just wanted to get it over with and get what was his and leave.

Casey nodded at Mark to start the video back up. Mark looked at everyone else in the room as if to see that they were all right with everything. "Okay, let's get back to this so we can get this done today. I know all of you have things to do." Cassie made a grunting noise, but she didn't say anything.

Once again Ben was on the screen, telling his story. "I didn't always get dressed every day, but for some reason I did that day. I didn't feel like turning the TV on. I was just sitting and going through some old pictures that Annie put in books. I did that a lot. Then I heard a car in the woods. I sat and listened, and it was around where Annie was. Then I heard car doors shutting and someone yelling. It wasn't Tuesday, so it wasn't Daniel delivering groceries and mail. And it wasn't Friday, so it wasn't Sara coming to check on me and bring the mail. Besides, they would have driven all the way up to the parking area."

Once again Cassie interrupted as she turned toward Sara and Daniel, "How much did he pay you guys a week to come out there. I bet you racked him over the coals. If there's no more money left, there's no sense in me sitting here and listening to all this."

John, Sara's husband and Daniel's father, spoke up on their behalf. "He only paid for the groceries and other supplies that he needed, like medication. I own a store in town, and we also have a pharmacy in it. We would let him give Daniel a tip, and that's all. We loved your father and your mother when she was alive."

You could tell Carrie was done listening to what he had to say. "Yea, yea, yea, I know who you are and your store. Your father owned it when we were kids. Let's get back to the movie."

This time Mark had to speak up. "Cassie, we just can't have you constantly interrupting the video, or we'll never get through with this. Could you and your brother please step into the other room for just a moment?"

While they were gone, Daniel came over to talk with the girls, mainly to Carissa. The spouses of the twins left because one of them wanted to step out and smoke a cigarette. Deidre moved over and started speaking to John and Sara. John wasn't very pleased and didn't want to be there in the first place.

"I don't need anything from Ben. They can have it all, but the lawyer said no one would get anything unless everyone was present. So I came just for those two ungrateful brats. Cassie was always bitter and downright mean. Casey always defended her, but you could tell he really didn't agree with her and wanted to be different. But Cassie controlled him. Now that I'm here and this is all going on, I don't care if they don't get anything. I'm done with all this. I need to get back to the store."

Right then Mark and Casey walked into the room, but Cassie wasn't with them. "Could everyone please take their seats please?" Casey's spouse was there, but not Cassie's spouse. "June, my assistant, will be in here in just a second and will be handing out a form for each of you to read and sign. It is agreeing that no one minds if Cassie doesn't have to continue watching the video but can still receive her inheritance."

Everyone was mumbling about how they had no problem with that— all accept one person, André. "Grandma, that's not what Ben wanted. It was very important to him that Cassie and Casey heard everything he said. He wanted to make amends with them and wanted to let them know who he had become at the end. I can't sign that paper, I just can't. He told me how he felt, and I can't go along with this. I'm like everyone else. I don't want her here, but Ben does."

Deidre wanted to try to change André's mind, but she knew that just wasn't going to happen. So Deidre and André approached Mark so that André could explain the situation to him. "I was the one who was with Ben during the taping of this video. Besides what he is saying here, he shared with me a lot more about the past and what happened between his children and him. This video is mostly for the both of them. Actually it's all for both of them. He needed to make amends with them, and he knew he would never see them while he was alive. But that didn't stop him. He still wanted to let them know after he was dead how he felt. I'm sorry. We can't go on without her."

The three of them were startled when Cassie spoke up behind them. "What do you mean he wanted to make amends with us? What all did he tell you?" Cassie's tone was totally different; it was calmer and gentler.

André spoke as careful and gentle as she could so that she didn't get Cassie started in one of her rampages. "He knew that he was wrong in a lot of ways and that it was mostly his fault that you and Casey left and that Annie would have been better off if he would have at least updated the house more and added on to it. It haunted him that he didn't take any of you into consideration." There was a lot more to say, but it would take a lot of time. And André knew everyone was waiting. "If you would like to talk later, I can tell you everything he said."

Everyone heard what André was saying, and the room stood silent as everyone wanted to hear Cassie's response. Cassie was looking down, and in the softest voice that anyone had heard from her since they all met, she said, "I would like that, and I'd like to join everyone and continue watching the video. I promise if something really upsets me, I'll leave the room until I compose myself."

June walked in with the forms and was about to pass them around, but then Mark stopped her. "Is everyone willing to have Cassie rejoin us? It's what Ben wanted." Everyone agreed. Some were a little less enthusiastic than others, but they all agreed.

André turned to return to her seat when Cassie touched André's arm. Then she turned back to Cassie. "For the life of me I don't understand, but I think you really had feelings for the old man, didn't you?"

André smiled gently. "I loved Ben very much. He was like my grandfather."

Everyone was seated and ready to continue with the video. Cassie now was ready to watch it in a whole new perspective. Deidre couldn't help but smile as she looked at her granddaughter. André never ceased to amaze her. It was time to get back to Ben.

"I slowly made my way to the porch and sat down to try to figure out what in the world was going on. I wasn't really afraid, so I didn't go get my rifle. I just listened. I heard a lot of rustling, and I could hear people saying things. But I couldn't understand what it was that they were saying. I couldn't see them because so much had grown up between the house and Annie's place, and there were trees and tree limbs that had fallen to the point that I could no longer walk to her place. I use to be able to see the sunlight pierce through the trees and shine on her place, but that was a long time ago. Then it was quiet for a while, but I knew they were still there because I didn't hear the car start and leave. I suddenly heard a women's voice yell out the name André. The voice of another woman yelled back, and I realized she was just on the other side of my barn."

Deidre enjoyed listening to Ben's side of the story of their meeting. She once again looked over at her granddaughters, and she noticed André was looking at some papers she had brought with her. She had asked her on the way to the hearing that day what the papers were, and she just said they were notes. Deidre also noticed that André was writing a lot in the notebook that day. She thought to herself, *"Could she be writing a story or maybe a book?"* There goes her imagination again. She went back to listening to Ben's story.

I thought to myself, "N*ow why are these women in my woods, and what would they possible want here? It's just a dead place with an old man waiting to die."* Then I heard the other women yell again for André, and André yelled back and tried to describe where she was. I could tell when they were together because I could hear them talking. I couldn't really hear what they were talking about, but I knew they were about to leave, so I decided to yell for them. I wanted to know who they were and why they were there. Besides, it would be nice to have some company. I don't know why, but all of a sudden, my day seemed a lot brighter than it had been in a long time. And I didn't even know who these people were.

CHAPTER 4

As Deidre started listening to Ben, she once again started remembering their first meeting.

When they heard someone yelling, "Hey there," Deidre grabbed Carissa's arm, and André grabbed Carissa's other arm. They stood there, quietly listening to see if they would hear the voice again. Deidra wasn't sure what they would do if they heard it again. Would they hurry and leave or meet the person who was calling out to them.

The voice called out again, "Hey, who's out there?" Then there was a pause. "Come on over and around the barn and let me see you." They could tell it was an elderly man's voice.

Carissa whispered to her grandmother. "We should go and at least explain why we're on their property. Besides, it sounds like some old man."

André wasn't sure she agreed with Carissa. "That old person might be looking down a barrel of a rifle."

Deidre took in a big breath and agreed to go take a peek but only on one condition. "We go slowly and cautiously. We have to check everything out as we go. If any of us see any kind of a weapon, fall on the ground and crawl back this way as quick as you can. I can't believe I'm doing this. Your grandfather is going to kill me when he finds out what we're about to do."

Carissa had a quick response to their question if he had a gun of some kind. "If we come, are you going to shoot us?"

André covered her month so that no one could hear her laugh. "I don't believe you just said that Carissa. He's not going to tell you that he has a gun."

Deidre was getting a little upset with the girls. "This isn't some funny game we're playing. You both need to get serious here. I think we just need to get back to the car and leave. I can't take any chances that you two might get hurt." Even though the girls really didn't want to leave, they knew that they had to respect their grandmother's wishes, so they all three tuned to start heading back to the car.

"I have a rifle but not with me. Why? Are you dangerous?" Both of the girls covered their mouths because they were laughing this time.

Deidre was going to end this now. "We're sorry, sir, that we were trespassing. We're leaving now."

The man spoke softer this time. "Please don't leave. I noticed you were at my Annie's place. Can you tell me if her place still looks okay?"

The three of them looked at one another. "Annie's place? Does he mean her grave, Grandma?" André was starting to feel very sad for the old man. "Okay, we're coming."

Deidre was shocked that André said that without even discussing it with her. "Come on, Grandma. I think that's why we're really here … for him." André didn't even wait for her grandmother's response. She just started to walk toward the barn.

Deidre thought that maybe she might be right and started following her, but she still didn't like the way André had defied her. "We still have to be very careful … *please.*"

The barn was big, and you could tell it hadn't been used in some time. It was still strong, but it needed paint and some boards replaced on the side. And it could use a new roof because it was sagging in places. The brush around the barn was high. They were all glad they had jeans and tennis shoes on because some of the weeds and grass came up to their thighs. When they got to the corner of the barn, they peeked around it and could see another shack-like building that was also in bad shape. On the other side of the shack, they could see some of the house. It was two stories, but that was all they could tell from there.

André was no longer leading. She felt safer behind her grandmother. "Oh, now you're no longer brave? You know I'll be the first one to get shot."

André knew her grandmother was kidding. "Oh Grandma."

Deidre stepped up the pace a little bit until they got to the smaller shack, which was about hundred feet or more away from the barn. She looked back at the girls before she checked around the corner. The girls were bending over, looking up at her their eyes open as wide as they could open them. Deidre couldn't help but smile. She slowly looked around the corner of the shack. She was surprised by what she saw.

The house was old and needed painting, there was a porch that was sagging and packed with stuff. There was ivy that was growing up the side of the house next to the chimney, but it was what was in front of the porch that surprised her. There was a beautiful flower garden with a large variety of flowers with a few garden statues in it. At the end of the porch was a large bush with red flowers. A few feet away from the garden, there was a tulip tree in full bloom. It was all so beautiful and well taken care of.

Deidre spotted an elderly man sitting on the edge of his rocking chair, looking at her. He motioned to them to come as he said, "Come on up. Don't worry. I'm the only one here, and as you can see, I'm no threat to nobody."

André started walking past her grandmother until Deidre grabbed her arm and pulled her back behind her. Deidre then started walking slowly up to the house as the two girls followed behind her so closely that André stepped on her grandmother's heel. "Sorry, Grandma."

Deidre didn't even respond to André because she was so engrossed in looking at everything around them. She decided they needed to apologize to the man for trespassing and intruding on him. "We're so sorry for trespassing and intruding on your privacy. We'll just head back out, and we promise you'll never see us again." Even though that was what she said, it wasn't what she wanted to do. For some strange reason, she wanted to stay and visit for a while, maybe look around and even take some pictures. But she knew they had already done more than they should have.

The man stood up, and Deidre could tell he had trouble getting around. "Before you leave, why don't you all come on up and visit just a little bit? I'd like to ask you a few questions if you don't mind."

They were trespassing and intruding, and he was hoping they'd stay awhile and visit? Slowly the three of them walked up to where the flower garden was. They couldn't help but stop and look at everything that was planted and obviously cared for with a lot of love. "Aren't Annie's flowers beautiful?" All three of them smiled and nodded yes to him. "Well, come on up. I'm sure we can find a seat for all of you. Do you want something to drink?" Deidre and Carissa said no at the same time while André said she'd like that.

The elderly man waited for them to step up on the porch, and he found a seat for each of them. Deidre had a chair. Carissa sat on a wooden crate, and André sat on a large wooden spool. The man excused himself as he went inside to get André something to drink. They could see it might take awhile since he didn't seem to be walking very well. Deidre slightly scolded André. "We have plenty of drinks in the car, and we're not going to be here that long. You shouldn't have made him go get you something to drink. He seems to be having a lot of difficulties walking."

André spoke softly so that the man wouldn't hear her. "I could tell he wanted to do something for us. People like to get something for their company. I read that somewhere."

The man was back way sooner than they thought he would be. The kitchen must have been close by.

The man handed the drink to André. "Here you go, missy. My name is Ben. What are all your names?" Each of them introduced themselves. The man continued to talk as he walked back to his rocking chair and slowly sat down. "Well, I wasn't expecting company, especially as pretty as you three. Now tell me what brought you my way, and did I hear you around Annie's place?"

Just as Deidre was about to speak, the two girls started talking at the same time, telling Ben everything, including spending the night with their grandmother and everything they had done that day up to the point when they came to his property. Then they stopped. At one point as they were talking, Ben looked at Deidre, and all she could do was shrug her shoulders and smile. He returned her smile and continued to listen to the girls. When they stopped, they looked over at their grandmother as if waiting for her to tell the part about being on his property and the grave they had found.

Ben gently urged them to continue. "And when you got here, how did you happen to find Annie's place?"

It was now Deidre's turn to tell the rest of the story. "I was compelled to turn onto your property. Please don't ask me why. I don't know why. It just happens sometimes."

Ben interrupted her, "You mean you do this kind of thing a lot?"

Deidre was hoping he wasn't getting upset. "No not really. Just once in a great while, something will strike me to pursue something I feel or see."

André felt she had to interrupt just this once. "You could say she's a little psychic."

Deidre assured Ben that wasn't the case, and she gave André a look that said *hush*. She continued to gently and cautiously continue her story. "After a few minutes, I started to look for an area wide enough so I could turn around, and suddenly I saw the sun striking through the trees and shining on something. We got out of the car to see what it was, and we found—I take it—your wife's grave."

Before she could continue, Ben bolted out, "I call it her place, not a grave. That sounds so cold. Tell me— How does her place look? Please don't tell me it's awful, but I guess it is awful because I can no longer see anything from here. It's all overgrown. Is her stone okay. It's not broken or gone, is it?"

Deidre now understood why Ben wanted them to talk to him. He wanted to know all about the love of his life, his Annie's place. It was obvious to her that it meant a lot to him. "The stone is just fine. The area was a mess. A tree had split in half and was lying over the stone, but we cleaned and picked everything up." She really didn't want to mention that they had taken pictures.

Ben was once again sitting on the edge of his rocker, and he now had a confused look on his face.

"Why did you do that? I mean, I'm very grateful, but why would you clean everything up and move that tree when you didn't even know her. You didn't know my Annie, did you?"

Deidre looked down and then slowly looked up at Ben. "No, we never knew your Annie. There was just something about the way the sun beamed on her place that—"

Carissa finished telling Ben what seemed to be too hard for her grandmother to say. "We felt that someone needed us to do it. And I hope you don't mind, but it was so beautiful there that we took pictures. All three of us are into photography. I'm taking a class in college for it."

Deidre thought for sure Ben was going to go off on them. She wasn't upset with Carissa, but she sure wished she hadn't mentioned that they had taking pictures. It completely surprised her when Ben's reaction was completely opposite of what she had expected.

"Pictures? Oh, how I wish I could see those pictures. When you have them developed, could you bring them by for me to see?"

Carissa stood up and moved toward Ben. "I can do better than that. I can show them to you right now. I have some before we cleaned up and after." She started showing Ben the pictures on her camera. At first his face was sad, and he just kept shaking his head. Carissa assured him that the pictures got better. As she continued, Ben started to smile. His eyes sparkled, and his whole face glowed.

That was the first time Deidre noticed his clear, bright blue eyes. Then she started noticing everything about him. He had streaks of black in his white hair. His face was aged with deep lines. He was thin but not skin and bones. And now she could see his smile. What a great smile. "*Someone must be coming and taking care of things for him*", she thought. "*Like caring for that lovely garden.*" She couldn't see Ben being able to do any of that.

Carissa sat back down, and everyone was quiet of a moment. André got up and walked over to Ben. She stooped down and took his hands. "Since were here, would you like for us to take you to Annie's place." Deidre was a little shocked. She had no idea how André thought they would be able to do that. The road didn't even come all the way up to the house.

Ben took a deep breath and sighed. "I have no way of getting out there any longer. The trail that's over there has become so bad, and some of it I don't think is even there any longer. It's all overgrown. There are trees and rocks, and I can hardly walk in the house, let alone out there."

With her ever-so-gentle and soft voice, André encouraged Ben, "I believe with all my heart that we were guided here to meet you and to take you to see Annie's place. Please trust us. Do you have a wheelchair or a walker that can help us get you there? We really want to do this for you." She never once looked back to see if her grandmother or cousin agreed with her.

"I have a wheelchair, but there's no way it can make it there. I hate that thing. I have a walker that I use when I have to go somewhere, but I don't think I can walk that far with the condition the trail is in. I just don't think it'll work - Missy." Ben's voice sounded so defeated.

André got up and started walking into the house. "Where's the walker? I know with our help you can do this."

Ben and Deidre got up the same time. Deidre couldn't believe how her granddaughter was acting. Carissa's face was in shock, but Deidre stopped her when she was about to say something. Ben and André came walking out with Ben's walker. Ben seemed to have more of a spring in his step, but he was still not sure of all this.

The four of them discussed how they were going to accomplish this together. Deidre explained, "The four of us are going to walk as one—step by step, inch by inch. We're not in a hurry, and when we have to move something, we need to find a place for Ben to rest." Everyone agreed, but you could tell by the expression on their faces, they weren't quite sure what it all meant.

As they started out, Ben kept shaking his head. "I just don't understand why you are going through all this just for me. It makes no sense."

Carissa just snickered and joked around. "That's just how we are, Ben. Things don't have to make sense for us to do it. Isn't that right, André?" André knew Carissa was referring to them being there in the first place.

There were times when they thought it wasn't so bad, but then there were a couple of broken trees and places where the brush was so high that it took some time to figure out how to get past. Deidre thought it was amazing how they would find a large rock for Ben to sit on whenever he needed to rest. "I remember this rock. When my health started going bad and I would walk out here, this was a good resting spot of me. I guess it's still a good resting spot."

Ben had some color in his cheeks, and he became more and more determined to make it, even though he was getting more and more tired. When they were getting closer, Ben had to put his arms around Deidre and Carissa's shoulders, and they carried him. André walked ahead of them, clearing the way and carrying the walker.

Deidre saw the sunbeams shining through the trees and knew they were really close, and so did Ben. "I think I can walk with my walker the rest of the way. I'd like to be standing on my own when we arrive at Annie's place." It took them close to an hour to get there, but seeing Ben's face when he saw Annie's place made every minute worth it. Ben shouted as if he had just arrived at an old friend's house. "Hi there, Annie. Here I am. Sorry it's been so long since I've been here. I had some help from some friends to come visit you. Everything looks real nice, doesn't it, Annie?

These ladies here cleaned everything up and then brought me here." There was a large rock next to the grave site that Ben sat on while he talked to her. Deidre gently guided the girls off a ways so that Ben could be alone.

"Grandma, since we're so close to the car, can I go get some food and something to drink. I'm starving, and I'm dying of thirst." André agreed with Carissa, and Deidre thought it was a good idea herself.

"Why don't you bring all the food and the cooler? We'll have a picnic out her with Ben." She didn't hear any arguments out of them, and they were back with everything in no time.

They walked up to Ben and showed them the picnic. "Oh, how great. Annie use to just love picnics, didn't you, Annie?"

After they were done, it took a while to get Ben to the car, but it was still better than going back the way they had come. He showed them how to follow the small road to an area where you could park the car and then walk a short distance to the house. Once they got him settled back into his house, they started saying their good-byes.

"Ben, before we leave, can I take a picture of you and some pictures of your house and the barns and that beautiful garden?" Deidre was hoping Ben didn't think Carissa was stepping out of line or being rude.

Ben was quiet for so long that Deidre was sure he didn't like the idea. "I don't know why you want those picture, but how could I ever say no to my three angels? God sent me three angels, but you can only take those pictures if you promise you'll come back to see me soon. I promise you won't have to take me to Annie's."

Carissa shook Ben's hand and proceeded to take lots of pictures until her grandmother said it was time to leave. They told Ben good-bye and started walking to the car. When they were halfway to the car, André turned and ran back and said something to Ben and then hugged him. When she returned, Deidre was going to ask her what that was all about but decided against it, and surprisingly Carissa did the same thing.

Everyone was very quiet on the way home. They were worn out, and it had been a long day. Right when Deidre thought both girls were asleep, André asked her, "Grandma, what made you go down that road?"

Deidre looked in the rearview mirror at her and winked. "That's just the way I am. Things don't have to make sense for me to do it."

André laughed.

CHAPTER 5

Back in the lawyer's office, Deidre felt Carissa nudge her. "You all right, Grandma?" Deidre nodded yes and smiled.

Then she heard Ben talking about when he had first met them and how the two girls were both talking at the same time.

"All of a sudden, those two girls started talking at the same time, and I couldn't understand a word they were saying. I looked at their grandmother to see if she could understand anything, but all she did was smile, so I just guessed she didn't understand anything either. But you sure could tell that that grandma loved her babies."

Ben couldn't have been more right. She loved her babies very much. As she looked over at them, she noticed André watching Cassie. Then suddenly Cassie turned around to check them out … or at least look at André. Deidre couldn't tell what Cassie was feeling or thinking, but she noticed that André didn't give any kind of emotional look, not even a smile, which was very strange for André.

Deidre's attention went back to the video as she watched and listened to Ben talk about the long ordeal of getting him to Annie's place and the picnic. What he said next answered a question that she had had on her mind for a long time.

"I couldn't believe my ears when André ran back to me and said not to worry, that I would be seeing a lot of them in the future. Then she hugged me and was off like an angel with wings."

The things Ben said next Deidre had never known or heard before, so she became very engrossed.

"At that moment life came back into my life. I had something to look forward to, and I decided there were things I needed to get done around the old homestead. I called the Matthews, who own the corner store, and talked to John and asked if he and his son, Daniel, could fix my steps and clear a better path to where the cars parked. They even built me a ramp, and I didn't even ask them to do that. I also talked to Sara, John's wife, and asked if she could help me clean my house a little. She's wanted to tackle my house for years. You remember the Matthews, don't you, Cassie and Casey?"

For the first time in a while, Cassie made a comment. "How could we forget? They always thought they were so much better than us when we were kids." Luckily everyone ignored her and her comment.

Ben continued talking about the work that had been done and then how he waited for the girls' return. "After a couple of weeks, I was starting to think they may not be coming back after all. Then the next thing I knew, there was André walking up the path, carrying lots of things in her hands and smiling from ear to ear. Boy did this old heart of mine soar like and eagle."

André remembered that first visit back to Ben's house. She thought she knew the way there, but she took the wrong exit and got lost. But she remembered what her grandmother always said. "If you do get lost, it won't be for long." It seems her grandmother was right because she was only lost for about thirty minutes.

When she found Ben's place, she was surprised that the path from the car to the house had been cleared away a lot. It made it a lot easier to carry all the things that she had brought. She had some items to cut Ben's hair and shave him, and she had also brought new clothes. She had some pictures she had developed from the first time they had been there too. She knew Carissa had a lot of pictures, but she wasn't sure when Carissa would be coming back again. She had talked to her earlier in the week, but Carissa couldn't come because she had such a busy schedule with school and her jobs. Carissa worked as an art tutor to children and also worked at a restaurant. André had a little more time on her hands. She had a few classes and only babysat part-time and helped her grandmother when she had an event to shoot. She had asked her grandmother what she was doing, but she was busy too. She didn't tell her grandmother she was coming because she was afraid she would try to talk her out of coming, but she had to come. Ben had been on her mind constantly since she had met him.

"Hi, Ben. Wow, everything looks nice. I like the path, and wow, look at these new steps. You've been busy." She knew there was no way Ben had done all this. She doubted very much that he had done any of it.

"Yeah, that's me. Just as busy as a bee." They both laughed as she stepped onto the porch. "What all do you have there, Missy?" He was trying to see what she had in the box she was carrying.

"Well, I'm hoping you'll let me play beautician and cut your hair. And I was going to tie you up and shave you, but you already look like you've had a shave. And I found some clothes I really like, and I thought you might like to try them on." She was talking as fast as she could before he could interrupt and refuse her fussing over him.

"Cut my hair? Do you know how to cut hair? And I have lots of clothes." Then he noticed something else in the box. "Are these pictures from when you were here the last time?" He started to get them out of the box, but André stopped them.

"No, no, no, you don't get to see the pictures until we cut your hair and put these fancy duds on. You may have lots of clothes, but do you have new clothes? And look how cool these are."

In the video Ben was commenting on how he felt about André's visit. "I didn't care what she wanted me to wear. I didn't even mind her cutting my hair. I was just so happy to have her there. I remember how I couldn't wait for her to come in the house and see what Sara had done with the place."

It was time for another comment from Cassie. "I can't imagine that it looked like anything but a dump with stuff moved around and out of the way."

André was tired of all the trouble Cassie was causing. "It looked nice and clean, and he was proud of it. I always liked his little house."

Cassie turned all the way around so that she could look André straight in the eye. "That's easy for you to say. You didn't have to live in that dump all your childhood days with everyone you know whispering behind your back about you being a misfit."

The argument would have continued, but Deidre, Casey, and Mark all three stopped it so that they could continue. Cassie turned around as if she was all proud of herself. André slumped back in her chair, her arms crossed, wearing a pouty face, but once she heard Ben's voice on the video, she started to remember once again that day.

"Let's cut your hair outside so that we won't make a mess in your house now that it's all cleaned up. I also brought us some pop. Do you like pop?" Ben told her sure and wanted to know if she had any hard stuff to put in the pop because he was going to need it after he went through everything that André was going to do to him. André gave him a scolding but kidding look, and they both laughed.

The afternoon was great. They laughed and shared stories. Ben even liked his haircut. André had him try on the clothes that she had brought, and when he came out, she fussed and fussed over him. Even though the clothes didn't fit quite right, he still looked nice. Ben pranced around like a young stud.

"Now since I'm all dudded up, I think we need to put on some music, and maybe you'll do me the honor to dance with me." He didn't wait for an answer. He walked in the house. Close to the door, there was a record player that he started up. When he came out, André couldn't help but smile because of how happy he looked. It wasn't much of a dance, because Ben couldn't stand very long, let alone dance, but it was a dance André would never forget. And neither would Ben.

Cassie couldn't take anymore. "Okay, I've had enough for now. Can we take a lunch break? This is making me sick to my stomach." Mark was about to say no when Deidre and John both agreed that it was a good idea. John needed to check in at the store, and others wanted to take a smoke break. Deidre was a little hungry so she knew the girls were probably starving. As Cassie passed André, she couldn't help but make a comment to her.

"I don't know how dancing with you has anything to do with that old man being sorry for what he did to me and my family." Then she continued to walk away, but André needed to put her two bits in.

"It doesn't have anything to do with you. That's the whole point." Cassie was about to walk back to André when Casey grabbed her arm and spoke to her. Then they continued on.

Mark asked André if they could talk in his office while everyone was out. André looked at her grandmother, and her grandmother told her she'd bring her something back to eat. Deidre and Carissa went to lunch with the Matthews, which made Carissa happy because she wanted to spend some time with Daniel.

After everyone left, Mark offered André a pop, which she accepted. While he was gone, André checked over the notes she had been writing. "I don't know if this is going to work, Ben. You really have a mean and spiteful daughter. But I'll keep on trying."

Mark handed her a pop and sat down at his desk. André was sitting in a chair on the other side of his desk. "André, I haven't watched this tape before today. Ben just kept telling me that it was very important that all of you see it, and he was very demanding that no one gets anything if they don't watch it. As you can tell, it's taking a lot more time than any of us expected. I don't think we're going to get it done today, and I have to be in court tomorrow. Since you know what's in this tape, can you tell me anything that would indicate that we really need to continue with the tape? Is it really going to change anything when it comes to everyone's inheritance?

André was afraid this was what the lawyer wanted to talk to her about. "Everything that is about to be given away to everyone was once Ben's. So if it belongs to Ben. Then Ben has a right to say his piece before giving anyone anything. I will tell you that Ben was concerned that something like this might happen. Maybe not this bad, but he felt something might happen. He doesn't want to just make amends. He wants to explain why each person is getting what they are going to get. You see, Mr. Talbot, Cassie and Casey aren't going to like what is about to happen."

Mark sat quietly for a moment, tapping his pen on his desk. "I know what's in the will, André, and I really don't think it's going to be as bad as you think. They're both going to receiving a good sum of money, more than I think they're expecting, and from what I've heard from them, they don't want anything to do with the house or anything in it. Since Ben has more or less put you in charge of the tape, can we agree that if it doesn't go any better this afternoon, we can jump over certain parts that might not make a difference one way or the other? Do you know what I'm trying to say?"

André looked down at her notes as if she was talking to Ben once again. Then she came up with an idea that she hoped Mark would agree to. "What if you tell everyone when they get back that if we don't get through this tape this afternoon, you won't be able to meet with them again for a week because of your court case? Maybe that will shut Cassie up. The only thing is the tape is rather long, so it will still take some time to get through it. I really don't want to jump over anything no matter how insignificant everyone may think it is."

Mark really had no choice but to agree. "Do you have any idea of how much longer this tape is—that is, without any interruption?"

"I'm guessing about a little over an hour. The whole tape should have taken about two hours at the most to watch. So you see, if Cassie keeps it up, we won't be done until late." André couldn't see Cassie keeping her month shut that long. Plus the smokers would want another break, so they were looking at maybe as much as three more hours or more.

That still wasn't as bad as Mark thought it was going to be when André said there was still a lot more of the tape to see. "Isn't there any way possible that Cassie can sit out in the waiting room until the tape is over? She won't be allowed to leave the office. She'll just wait out front."

André was beginning to feel defeated. "Let's just see what happens after you talk to everyone, and if things still go bad this afternoon, we'll reconsider what to do with her."

André was happy to see her grandmother step into the office. She was emotionally drained over all this, and she was starving.

Deidre could tell her granddaughter was exhausted. "Here. You need to eat something. Carissa is with the Matthews, and they'll be back shortly. Mark, is it all right if she eats in the waiting room?"

Mark looked up from some papers he was going through. "Sure, no problem. She'd probably like a change in scenery." He gave them a weak smile and started looking over his papers again. "Oh, by the way, thank you, André, for staying and helping me try to figure things out. I really appreciate it."

Once they were in the waiting room, Deidre asked André if she was all right and if there was anything she could do to help. André took a bite from her hamburger and sat back in her chair. "Yeah, you wouldn't have any ketchup, would you?" Deidre hugged and kissed her on the cheek and reached in the bag to get the ketchup.

Everyone returned and took their seats. Carissa sat with Daniel off by themselves. They sat in the back of the room across from André and Deidre. André had to make faces at Carissa to tease her and maybe embarrass her a little.

Mark wasn't in the room when everyone arrived. When he entered, he smiled at everyone and hoped for the best. He told everyone what he and André had discussed, but he didn't let them know it was André's idea. It went just as badly as Mark had thought it would. Cassie and Casey were both on their feet, ranting and raving. Even John opposed the idea. Mark had to raise his voice so that they could hear him. "I'm saying this will only happen if we don't get through the tape. So Cassie, if you can refrain from commenting all the time and constantly stopping everything, we will get this done today, but that will be the only way it will get done. It's all up to you."

Casey and Cassie looked at each other, and Cassie slowly sat down. Casey then asked a favor. "Can I have just a few minutes with Cassie in the other room? I promise it will only be just a few minutes." Mark agreed, and Casey took Cassie's hand and led her to the other room. After about five minutes, they were back and took their seats. Casey told Mark to continue the tape. No one could tell anything from the expression on Cassie's face.

Deidre thought it was strange that Cassie's husband never once tried to control her or calm her down. It was always Casey who did all that. All Cassie's husband would do is sit and look straight ahead or look at the lawyer, but never once did he look at Cassie or anyone else really.

At the moment June, Mark's assistant, came in and whispered in his ear. You could tell by Mark's face that it wasn't good news. Mark hated doing this. But it was about the case he had the next day, and it was vitally important. "I will be right back. This shouldn't take long at all."

As Mark was leaving the room, he could already hear Cassie saying, *"Are you kidding?* After all that talk about me, and he ups and leaves and delays everything. Well, all I have to say is he'd better not make it so that we have to wait a week before we can complete all this."

Under André's breath she couldn't help herself. "That would be great if that's all she has to say." The only one who could hear her was her grandmother, who just had to snicker.

Cassie couldn't hear what André said. But she could hear her mumbling, and she heard Deidre snicker. "What's so funny? Are you making fun of me?"

Without causing trouble but not lying, André's comeback was very clever. "Not everything is about you." That seemed to satisfy Cassie.

Mark was back surprisingly soon. "I don't want to hold everyone up any longer than needed, so I'm going to start the tape back up. I'll finish my call, and I'll be right back." Everyone agreed to that solution, especially Cassie, and Mark started the tape and slipped out of the office.

CHAPTER 6

When the tape started, Ben was talking about how when André left, she said she'd be back in a couple of weeks. That was why he was surprised by what happened. "About three days later, I heard a car drive up the path and park. It sure took a long time to see that it was Deidre, and she had a box of stuff too."

Deidre remembered her first visit back to see Ben. She hadn't talked to André, so she didn't know at that time that she had come to visit Ben too. She also noticed how nice the path was from where the car was parked to the house. She stopped to look around and remember everything that had happened. She brought Ben a casserole, fried chicken, fresh fruit, and a mixed salad she had made up. She had also brought the pictures that she and Carissa had shot—not just the ones from Ben's place but the ones from the whole trip. There were five pictures so far that Carissa was hoping to enter in the showing, only if the art professor liked them.

As she was walking up to the house, she could tell some work had been done to the stairs. Then she saw Ben smiling from ear to ear as he watched her come closer.

"Hi, Ben, I hope you don't mind that I just dropped by without notice, but I don't have your phone number." She didn't know how he was going to react to her coming unannounced again, but by his smile, it must have been a good thing.

"It sure took you a long time to get out of your car, but it looks like you brought something, so I guess that's why. Come on up, and let's see what you have there."

When Deidre got to the porch, she showed Ben the box of food, and he led her into the house to put the food in the kitchen. As she was emptying the box, Ben couldn't believe how much food she had brought. "Are we going to eat all that food now? You really must be hungry."

Deidre chuckled and explained to him that it was for him for different days, but she thought they might have the chicken and salad if he was hungry. They had lunch and talked for a while. Deidre was in total shock when Ben told her about André's visit a few days ago. Why hadn't André mentioned it to her? Then she remembered André asking her what she was doing that day, but she thought André was just wondering if she had a shoot. She didn't like the idea of her coming here alone on her first visit. After all, they really didn't know Ben yet. She would talk to André later about this.

Deidre brought out the pictures and started showing them to Ben. She showed him the ones that Carissa was hoping to enter in the showing. Ben loved the graveyard with the tree and the church and even Annie's place, but he didn't know why in the world she would pick the picture of him sitting in his rocker as one of them. "Why would she want to enter a picture of an old man sitting in a rocking chair? I wasn't shaved, and I didn't have this nice haircut." He turned his head sideways, smiled, and stroked his hair.

Deidre thought to herself that he was a real character, but she really liked him. "I think she liked the characteristics in your face. It's like your face tells a story."

Ben interrupted, "Yeah, a really long story." Ben didn't want to talk about himself, so he asked Deidre if she would like to look around his property more.

Deidre wasn't sure what there was to see that she hadn't seen before, but she agreed. "Are you able to walk?"

Ben stood up and waved his hand at her as he reach for his walker. "Sure, we're not going very far, and I've been walking more lately. Plus look at this nice ramp that my friends built. They built those steps too along with clearing that path. I'm thinking I might have them come out and do some more work. They're really busy, so I don't know when it will be."

After they left the porch, Ben led Deidre to the side of the house opposite from where she had come in from the first time. The walk was difficult for Ben, but he was handling it okay. When they had cleared the side of the house, she was astounded.

"Oh, Ben, this is breathtaking, I had no idea this was here." Ben smiled. He knew she would fall in love with it. Not very many people would think it was much, but for some reason he knew she would fall in love with it. By looking at her pictures, he knew she knew what real beauty was.

There were trees around where they were standing, but just past them there was a clearing of land that led to a creek. On the other side of the creek, there was a beautiful stretch of land that had hilly fields with trees nestled here and there. You could see the creek winding around the hills. There were also two sections of land on each side that were farmed. One was a cornfield, and the other was a bean field. There were also some cows way off in the distance. You could see miles and miles away. Deidre just kept shaking her head and explaining how beautiful it was.

In a very soft and serene voice, Ben explained to her what she was looking at. "Everything you can see belongs to me." Deidre jerked her head toward Ben, but Ben just continued to look at the land and tell her all about it. "It's been in my family since my great-grandfather. I rent out some of the land to farmers to plant their fields, and that field way over there where the cows are is a field I rent out to a milk farmer. I sold some land way over on the other side of the barn when Annie became sick and we needed money. I thought about selling more land a couple of times since there's no one to leave it to, but there was no hurry. I've had some pretty good offers, but like I said, there's no big hurry. You used to be able to see all this from the back of my house, but it's all overgrown now to the point that you can't even see the creek."

Deidre's thoughts were disrupted by a comment from Cassie. "Glad someone liked that stupid land besides him. He should have sold all of it by now if he had a buyer." That's all she said, so it didn't stop or delay anything, but everyone was hoping they weren't going to hear anything from her. Oh well, wishful thinking. Deidre also noticed Mark wasn't back yet.

As Ben continued his story, Deidre remembered everything as if it was yesterday. As her and Ben walked back to the porch, she had to ask him, "You and Annie never had any children?"

Ben just kept walking without missing a beat. "Well, that's opening a whole new bag of worms."

By the tone of his voice, she was sorry she had said anything. "I'm sorry. I didn't mean to bring up anything that brought back any painful memories." She thought maybe a child had died, or even worse, maybe more than one.

Ben sat down in his rocker and asked Deidre if she could go inside and get them both some water. "My well's not so good, but I have some water in the refrigerator."

When Deidre returned, Ben asked if she had some time to talk a little while longer. She told him that she could stay a couple of hours longer and explained that her husband, Brad, was out of town and that there was no one else at home.

Ben started telling her about his family. "I have two children, twins. They don't care much for me, and they hate this place. When they were kids, I always liked to keep life simple. I still do now. They always wanted to be like everybody else. I was a strict father, and I don't think there's anything wrong with that. They had chores. All kids should have chores. I didn't like having a lot of kids around, so no friends stayed the night or came over after school. I was wrong for doing that. I know that now. I also wasn't big on buying lots of clothes or stuff. I made sure they had clothes, and they were good solid clothes. And they had food and a home. But they wanted stuff that just wasn't needed. They wanted me to change our home, and at one point they talked Annie into trying to get me to tear the house down and build a newer and fancier one. That's when things started to get hard between my kids and me. Annie seemed to understand how I felt about the history of our home and land, but those kids just worked on her all the time ... and on me a lot. They always thought everyone looked down on them. They just needed to quit worrying about what everyone else thought. They had a good life and didn't even know it. But now when I look back, I wish I would have done a few things different, you know, to make them happier ... and Annie too. But I just don't know if anything I would have done would have made a difference."

All of a sudden, the tape stopped. Mark had stopped it because Cassie was crying, and he was giving her a moment to go to the restroom. "Does anyone else want to take a break? Only five minutes please." Everyone left except Carissa and Daniel.

André wasn't sure what was up, but she couldn't imagine that Cassie was that upset. She slowly stepped into the restroom, but there was no Cassie. She stepped outside where the smokers were, but there was no Cassie. She decided to walk around the building, and she found her at the back of the building—or at least she heard her. She was talking to someone on her phone, explaining how upset she was and that there was no way she was going to be able to meet them. She was quiet and then said, "I love you too, sweetheart, and I miss you. Remember once this is all over, I'm going to dump that deadbeat husband of mine, and then I'm all yours."

André was shocked at what she had just heard but didn't put it past her. She decided to let her know she was there. "Oh, there you are. It's time to get back. We don't want to make everyone wait now, do we?" Cassie was startled by André's appearance, but André didn't give her a chance to say anything. She turned and headed back to the office. Everyone was getting seated by the time André came in. She sat down quickly and then watched for Cassie to come in. Cassie was the last one in, and she stopped for just a second to glare at André. André just smiled back.

When she looked over at her grandmother, all her grandmother said was, "I don't even want to know." But André assured her she was definitely going to fill her in later.

When they got back to the tape, Ben was talking about Annie. "I feel that Annie deserved more than the twins ever deserved. That's where I failed the most. Annie loved it here, and she really didn't mind the house except for when those kids started on her."

In the office, they constantly heard grunting noises from Cassie, but Casey made sure nothing else came out of her mouth.

Everyone continued to listen to what Ben had to say. "She was a good and gentle woman. She made everything so much fun like having picnics, picking fresh flowers from her garden, and putting them in the house. She would sing when she cleaned the house, when she sewed. She enjoyed going for walks in the woods. She loved sitting on the porch and singing along with the record player. We would all dance on the porch, me with Annie and Casey with Cassie. She's the one who was always trying to keep the peace between me and those kids." Deidre could see the flaw in what Ben had done in the past, but it didn't sound like things were all that bad.

She remembered Ben asking her to hand him the photo album that was sitting on a small metal table right behind her. She moved her chair next to his so that they could both see the pictures. The pictures seemed to be like any normal family—Easter, Christmas, picnics, school, the house. Then she noticed that Cassie never smiled in any pictures except her graduation picture. When she asked Ben about it, he told her what Cassie had said to him when they took the picture and noticed she was smiling.

"This is the happiest day of my life. I can now get out of this rat hole." She continued to tell them her plans. "Casey and I have made arrangements to leave today after graduation."

"Annie and I had planned on taking them out to dinner to a nice restaurant in town."

Cassie just laughed at us. "Why in the world would we want to spend a single minute more with you?"

"She apologized to her mother but blamed her for not standing up for them and always taking my side. Casey never said much, but he never did. He just always went along with Cassie, so I never asked him how he felt. After the graduation ceremonies, they already had their things packed and had called a taxi and were gone."

You could tell it was hard for Ben to talk about what had happened between him and his family. "Annie was never the same after that day. She hardly ever sang except in church, not even when she spent hours in her flower garden. She would dance with me on the porch sometimes, but she never acted like she enjoyed it as much. After a while we stopped dancing. We continued our picnics, but we didn't talk too much. We never talked about the kids. I know she got letters from them sometimes. But she never discussed them with me, and I didn't want to hear anything about them. I think hearing from them made things worse, because every time after she got one of those letters, she would be all sad and quiet. That only made me madder at those kids."

Deidre hated to interrupt him, but she needed to know something to better understand what Ben was saying. "Didn't you ever wonder what was in the letters, especially since you saw how Annie reacted after each letter? Did you try to find ways to help her get through everything she was feeling?" She was hoping she wasn't going too far with her questions.

Ben didn't like the questions, but he felt that if he was going to tell Deidre about his family, he had to expect she would have questions. She may not even like him after she heard what he was saying. He thought once about stopping, but he knew he'd gone too far to stop now. "Oh, I wondered a lot about those letters, but I was afraid if I knew what was in them, I would start yelling about those kids all over again. I did mention once to her that if those letters hurt her that much, she needed to stop writing to them. Then they would probable stop writing to her. She started crying and said that good or bad the letters were all she had left of them. That's when I decided to start doing more for my Annie. We started going to town more to have dinner and shop a little. We even went to the movies sometimes when it was cold or rainy. I had our house painted, and we bought some new furniture and updated our house with a microwave, new refrigerator, and stove. After a while she started perking up, but still not like the old Annie."

Deidre was happy to hear that Ben really did love his wife and tried to change things for her. She listened as he talked about how she started decorating the house more and then started making friends at church, and she became friends with the Matthews. They were John's parents, Jake and Mary. "She knew how to drive but never did until around then. She met friends for lunch and sewing groups. The Matthews invited us to dinner. I couldn't say I enjoyed it at first, but I sure loved watching Annie have fun. We went a couple of times a month. Then after a while I realized that I started looking forward to it. We started having picnics with them, and Jake helped me with the house and barns. We became close friends. Annie became alive again, and we started a new relationship. Too bad I didn't do it a lot sooner."

Ben continued talking about how their lives had changed and how active they had become in the community. It was mostly Annie, but he engaged in quite a few activities. It sounded like they had developed a good life for themselves.

It was starting to get late, and Deidre told Ben that she needed to start home. But before she left, she wanted to ask Ben something that had been on her mind. "Ben, you said something earlier about having your friends come over to do some more work around here. What all are you wanting to get done?"

Ben stood up so he could gesture as he talked. "I'd like a lot of this brush and the small trees cleared away and have that grass cut or cleared between the house, shed, and barn. And I'd like to have some more work done in the house. Sara, my friend, can only do so much at a time. There's a lot to do in that house. Since it looks like I might be having company more often, I might as well spruce up the place some. It's a nice place when it's fixed up."

Deidre suggested that it would be nice if some of her family could meet Ben's friends and help with the work around there. Ben didn't know what to think about the offer. "I don't know if I can pay all of you."

Deidre assured him that they wouldn't charge him. It was just a way to get to know him and his friends. Ben shook his head as he looked down. "I just don't understand you, Deidre. I've never known people like you. There's no reason for you to do any of this, yet you keep amazing me." They exchanged phone numbers, and he told her he'd get with the Matthews and set a time up when they could all get together. As Deidre was walking back to her car, Ben shouted out, "I said the last time I saw you and your babies that you were my angels." She looked back at him with a smile and saw him waving and smiling back.

CHAPTER 7

Everyone continued to listen to Ben as he talked about how he worked to get everyone together and how excited he was, not only because of the work that was going to get done but also because of the people coming over and meeting Deidre's family.

Deidre was curious about how quiet Cassie was. She could hear her once in a while whisper to Casey, but all in all she was really restraining herself from interrupting. She wondered if it had anything to do with what had happened earlier with Cassie and André. As she looked over at André, André looked back at her, smiled, and then went back to watching the video.

It was funny when Ben took breaks from videotaping because he would say to everyone, "Well, it's time for a break. You all go get something or do something, I'll be back." But there really wasn't any break in the tape. He'd come back on screen and say, "Well, let's get back to this movie. Now where was I?" And then he would laugh. You could hear André in the background getting Ben back on track, and he'd say oh yeah and start again.

Ben started telling about the day everyone got together and how great it was. Deidre agreed it was a great day and the start of new friendships and relationships. She loved thinking about it.

The day was warm. But there was a great breeze, and the trees helped shade everything. The Matthews arrived first, and they were going over everything with Ben as Deidre and her family arrived. They had driven four different vehicles, so they had to work to find places to park. The Matthews' truck was already there. Deidre was so excited for Brad to meet Ben. Her daughter, Marie, and her husband, Derrick, came in their truck. Marie was also André's mother. Marie's son, Ryan, rode with Deidre's son

Taylor in Ryan's small truck. André and Carissa rode together in André's car. Every vehicle was loaded up with the different types of supplies needed to do any kind of work that Ben might have had for them. Deidre had talked to Ben a number of times on the phone, and she finally got him to narrow down the work he really wanted done.

The family kept going on and on about how they could have found that place. Brad put his arm around Deidre and quietly spoke into her ear. "We need to talk tonight. I don't like what I'm seeing. I know you told me all about this place, and I was concerned. But I'm even more concerned now. You need to stop taking chances like this."

Deidre thought this might happen, but she knew Brad would understand as the day went by. She had to admit to herself that he was right. It was a big chance she was taking at the time, and she needed to be more careful—if not for her sake, then for the girls. As they all neared the house, André and Carissa noticed the Matthew family. They both noticed Daniel, John, and Sara's son.

After all the introductions, Ben went through what he'd like done outside first. He told them where they could find all the tools they would need. "I have no idea what shape the tools are in, but I had every tool and all the equipment needed to keep this place up." Then the guys were off. Ryan and Daniel seemed to hit it off right away, maybe because they were around the same age.

As they walked away, Carissa leaned over to André and commented, "Too bad I can't go help the guys, or should I say help Daniel?" André smiled and agreed with her.

Ben watched the girls for a minute as they were watching Daniel and then turned around to the ladies and shrugged his shoulders. "I'm not sure where to have you ladies start. Maybe Sara has an idea."

Sara took over from there, and they all went into the house, except for André. She stopped to give Ben a hug and talk to him for a few minutes. "You look great, and look how much better you're getting around. When we first met, you could barely walk into your house and back. Are you exercising?"

Ben perked up like a proud peacock. "I'm glad you notice. I've been walking around the yard and house every day to get my strength back. A while back when arthritis hit me in my hips, I just gave up, and so I just kept getting worse. I'm hoping to get strong enough that someday with just a little help, I can start going to visit Annie's place again. I won't make anyone go through what you girls went through that first time."

André put her arm through his arm and squeezed it. "We loved doing it for you. But it looks like it won't be any time at all when we'll take that walk to her place." Just then she got an idea.

André told Ben she needed to go. Ben was going to tell her she was going the wrong way, but he had a feeling she was doing exactly what she wanted. When she arrived at the shed, she met with Ryan, Daniel, and her uncle, Taylor. She wasn't sure what their plans were for the day, but she felt it was important to let them know about something really important that needed to be done.

"There's a trail that is in really bad condition that goes out to where Ben's wife is buried. He used to go out there a lot until the trail got so bad and the pain from his arthritis became so strong. He's been exercising so that he can start going back out there again, but I can't see how he can do that with the way it is. Is there any way that you guys could work on that? And maybe later when it's time, we can have a picnic lunch out there. That's one of his favorite things to do."

Taylor told her he wasn't sure what the others had planned but that he would have to get with them to find out what they thought, but he thought it was a great idea. "I know Ben wanted some brush and small trees cleared away from that general area. I guess we could just keep working down the trail. But like I said, I need to get with the others to see what's up."

André expressed once more how important it was and then headed back to the house. When she arrived, she didn't see Ben, which was good. She didn't what to have to explain to him why she went to the shed instead of the house. Inside everyone was cleaning, and Sara had brought new curtains, rugs, a bedspread, and few other new items. Just then Carissa came up and pushed a rag into her cousin's hand and commented about where she had been. "So did we take a little walk to check things out at the shed or maybe the barn?"

André smiled and looked around before she told her what she was up to. Carissa was thrilled over the idea and asked if she talked to Daniel. André told her, "I saw him, but I didn't talk to him. I just talked to Uncle

Taylor." Carissa gave her an "I'm not sure I believe you" look and then showed her what they were ordered to do.

A couple of hours later Daniel walked into the house and found André. "Your uncle wanted me to let you know that we're just about finished with the path. It should be done about two o'clock."

Before André could remark, Carissa jumped in. "That's so great. We'll start making some lunch and meet you guys out by the grave site at two. Is that okay?" Daniel nodded his head yes and started back out the door.

André softly put her hand on his shoulder before he could get out the door. "Ben doesn't like it called a grave site. He likes it called Annie's place, so tell the guys that, okay?" Daniel told her that he knew that and that he had already told all the guys.

The three older women walked out of the house at the same time with boxes, bags, and baskets of food. Ben assumed they were going to set up a place where everyone was going to eat. But they just kept walking into the woods. At the moment he was going to ask where they were going with all that food when André and Carissa walked up. Then André handed Ben his walker. "Time for lunch. Let's go."

"Go? Where are we going?" Ben was very confused, but knew he'd better obey, or he wasn't going to get any of that good-smelling food. André told him where there were going for lunch.

Ben stopped. "I don't think I'm ready to tackle that trail yet. There's just too much in the way, even though the boys cleared a little bit away up here in the front."

Carissa wondered how Ben didn't see that they had done a whole lot more than that. She was about to tell him that before André spoke up. "Oh, I think you can do a lot more than you think. I think you'll be surprised at how much easier it will be than you realize." Ben started shaking his head, but the girls wouldn't take no for an answer. "You don't want all of us to have a picnic at Annie's place without you, do you? Besides if you can't make it, we'll go get the guys to take you the rest of the way."

Ben still wasn't crazy about the whole idea because he remembered how hard it was the first time. "Don't you think if we take your car, it will be easier for everyone. We did that coming back the last time?"

Carissa looked at André. She didn't know how to respond to him. André knew exactly what to say to convince Ben. "Let's just call this a trial trip so that you'll know how far you are with being ready to do this someday by yourself." Ben wasn't sure he'd ever be able to do it by himself, but he sure liked the idea of being able to go anytime he'd like.

Ben took a deep breath, and they started down the trail. He realized quickly that a lot of work had been done to the trail. "Well, I'll be. What's happened here? When did this all happen? Oh, my goodness, it hasn't looked like this in— Gee, I don't remember how many years."

Carissa asked, "How did you not see that they were working farther than you had asked them to?"

Ben kept walking as he answered, "I started napping soon after I first saw them start working out here."

Ben only stopped to rest once on what he called the resting stone. When they entered the clearing of Annie's place, everyone started cheering for Ben. Deidre and Sara took Ben from the girls and seated him in a camping chair they had brought. They had camping tables, chairs, coolers, and even some music from a radio that Derrick had brought. Ben became overwhelmed by everything. Everyone became quiet when Ben slowly got up from his chair and walked over to Annie's stone. He rubbed the top of Annie's headstone as if he was rubbing her shoulder. "My, my, my, Annie, just take a look at this party going on. It's a real picnic, and they included you. I just don't know what to say." Then he bent his head down and wept."

CHAPTER 8

Ben continued talking about the different visits that each of the girls made. It was amazing how clear his memory was. "Do you remember, Deidre, when you, André, and Carissa came to paint the living room? At first I was wondering why you brought so many drop cloths, and then I understood when you three came walking out on the porch with paint all over you. I laughed so hard." As he laughed on the tape, Deidre and the two girls started laughing along with him.

Deidre remembered when she and Carissa took Ben to town for the first time. At first he wasn't sure he wanted to go, but at the end of the day, he loved it and couldn't stop talking about it all the way home. That's also when Carissa and Daniel became a lot closer.

Deidre thought Ben needed to get out of his surroundings, so when she told André and Carissa what she was planning, she asked if either one of them might want to go. Carissa jumped at the opportunity. André had to babysit to make some money.

On the way there, Deidre noticed how Carissa seemed overly anxious. "Where are we going to take him? Are we going to go by the Matthews' store?"

Oh, so that was what it was all about? Deidre remembered the day everyone went out to Ben's to work and how Carissa and Daniel sat next to each other during the picnic. They became very chummy. "Why would we go to the Matthews'?" When she looked over at Carissa, she could tell how disappointed she was, so she let her know she was kidding. "I was just kidding with you. Yes, that's one of the places we're going to. Sara has some groceries for him, and she had bought some couch pillows and a throw for his chair. Then I thought it would be nice to take Ben to dinner. Maybe the Matthews will go with us." That got a smile out of Carissa.

Deidre had called Ben to arrange the outing and had to persuade him to go. He kept coming up with excuses, and none of them were going to work on her. "I really don't need anything. And what I do need I just call the Matthews up, and they deliver it for me. Besides I'm still not really good at walking much. But you girls are more than welcome to come and visit."

Deidre didn't make any excuses up. She was open and honest and straight to the point. "Ben, it's time you get away from there. You need to spend time in the real world. Besides, I would rather do something with you than just sit and visit. As for walking, you and I both know you're doing just fine with that walker. Now do we come and take you to town or just skip the visit altogether?"

Ben wasn't used to being told what to do. "Boy, you can really be contrary, can't you? You don't like my company anymore?"

Deidre wasn't going to let him get away with something like that. "You know I love your company. I just want to enjoy it somewhere else besides just at your house."

Ben finally gave up. He admitted to her that he had met his match, and they both laughed.

When she and Carissa arrived, Ben was sitting on an old wooden box next to where everyone parked their cars. Deidre was hoping that it was a sign that he was more eager to go than he had let on to her on the phone. Carissa jumped out and helped Ben in the car and put his walker in the trunk of the car, and then she jumped in the backseat.

Ben didn't waste any time letting her know how he felt about this trip. "I had Daniel put that box there so that if I ever had to go somewhere, I could wait there for whoever was coming. Since I want to hurry up and get this done with, I thought we'd get a head start by you not having to come get me."

Deidre knew that two could play this game. "You're telling me that you're in that big of a hurry to get our visit with you over?"

Before Ben could answer, Carissa came to Ben's rescue. "I don't think that's what he meant, Grandma. He just doesn't want to go to town." Ben and Deidre looked at each other. They knew what each of them meant, and they laughed at what Carissa had said.

Their first stop was at the corner store, the Matthews' store. The moment they stepped out of the car, Daniel was there. He helped Ben out of the car and then turned to Carissa, and they started whispering to each other as they walked away together. Since Ben was there he decided to pick up a few more grocery items—well, a lot more. Deidre invited the family to go to lunch with them. John and Sara couldn't go, but when Daniel heard about it, he asked his mother if he could finish the work he was doing later and go with them. She smiled and looked at Deidre. "I don't mind if Deidre doesn't. She'd have to bring you back afterward." Deidre assured her that she didn't mind at all and said that she would pick everything up when she dropped Daniel off.

They didn't go anywhere fancy. Ben asked Daniel if Maggie's Diner was still open.

"Yeah, but different people own it now. But the food is the same. Plus they added a lot more to the menu." So they had dinner there, and Ben loved the food. Since it was such a great day, they decided to go to the city park and go for a small walk. The park was small but beautiful. Lots of different types of trees and flowers flowed throughout the park. There was also a winding sidewalk with benches every few feet or so.

Carissa and Daniel went for a walk alone. Deidre and Ben walked a short ways and sat down on a bench that was just across from a small play park. They sat quietly and watched children playing and parents watching their children.

While Ben was watching, he started talking about Annie. "Annie loved the park. We brought the twins here about twice a month when they were small and had picnics. Naturally everything is different. Now this play area is all new. We stopped coming when the kids decided they hated it, and Annie wouldn't make them come. Later after the twins left and Annie and I started doing things together, this is one of the things we started doing again."

Ben's voice changed as he spoke quieter, but he continued to watch the children play. "Then Annie started getting so tired. She kept making excuses and assuring me that she was just fine. She'd say things like how she just needed to eat better or that she just needed to start taking vitamins. I knew there was more to it, but I felt Annie would tell me when it was time to do something about it. And that's just what she did. We were setting on the porch late one afternoon, and she very calmly told me that she needed me to take her to the hospital. They said that it was stage-four cancer of the liver and that she had probably known about it for some time. When I asked her about it, she said she knew she was dying of something. But she didn't want to know what it was because she was tired of living, very tired. I took her home, and a couple of weeks later she wanted me to take her to this park, so we came here. It was fall and was very chilly outside, so there were no children playing. Besides wearing her coat, I took a blanket and wrapped her up really good. We hardly said a word to each other. She looked at me and told me she had always loved me. I put my arm around her and told her I had always loved her too. She said she wanted to go home, so we did. A couple of weeks later, she died at home in her bed. She didn't want to die in a hospital, so I didn't make her go."

Mark stopped the tape because this time Cassie was crying for real this time, and Casey was very emotional. Deidre had tears in her eyes the first time Ben told her this story, and she had tears in her eyes again this time.

Cassie, Casey, and their spouses left the room, and John came over and explained that this was the first time that the twins had heard the story of how their mother had died. They never knew any of the details of her death.

André exclaimed, "They didn't want to know. When Annie was dying, Ben called both of them, and they wouldn't call back, so he left a message on both of their answering machines saying only one thing, 'Your mother is dying.' But they still didn't respond. So I don't feel a bit sorry for them." Deidre was disappointed in André. She didn't like the idea of her feeling so bitter toward anyone.

Deidre noticed that Carissa and Daniel had left the room as well. André saw her grandmother looking over at where they had been sitting. "I'll go look for them, Grandma."

Deidre assured André that they were fine, but that didn't matter to André, as she jumped up to go find them. Deidre thought it was probably a good idea that she get up and move around a little anyway.

Everyone came back slowly, and the tape continued as Ben told his story. Ben talked about the funeral and how the twins came. They stayed in town, and he only saw them at the funeral and grave site. "They came up to me together like they always did. And Casey hugged me, but Cassie just asked questions about what I was planning to do now that Annie was gone, She thought I should sell everything and move into town since I was all alone. When I told her nothing had changed, she just got all mad and told me off again and told Casey she would wait for him at the car. Casey told me he was sorry about my loss, *my loss*. He sounded like a stranger or an acquaintance of some kind, nothing like a son. I was so glad Annie couldn't hear them."

You could hear Cassie occasionally saying something to Casey. But she didn't interrupt anything, and she didn't stop anything. Deidre was very grateful because she didn't think she would have been able to contain herself if Cassie would have said anything loud enough for her to hear.

Ben continued to talk about how his life had gone downhill from there. His spirit for life had diminished first. Then he became a recluse and never socialized in any way, not even at church. He revealed how he had everything delivered so that he wouldn't have to talk to anyone except the Matthews. He kept busy, but nothing had meaning any longer. He talked about how he visited Annie's place every day, sometimes twice a day.

Ben became sad as he continued telling this part of his story. "Time went by, and I no longer saw any reason to keep things up around the homestead. I was the only one there, and I no longer cared. The Matthews would deliver things and sometimes come check up on me. They volunteered to do some work around the place for me, but I told them I was planning on doing those things myself someday. I had no desire or plans on doing anything around the place. I think I wanted everything to die along with me."

Ben explained how he had a stroke that made walking and using his left side really difficult. "I was told to do some therapy exercise, which I didn't really do much of." Then he came down with pneumonia. "I wouldn't let them put me in the hospital. I just took the medicine they gave me, and Sara made sure I ate." He said a couple of times he broke a bone, one in his right leg and the other in his left arm. Then the arthritis set in on top of the leftover side effects from the stroke that he had had. It made getting around next to impossible. "No matter what happened to me, I just kept living. I was done with living, or at least I thought I was until I heard those angels' voices. All of a sudden, there was something inside me that wanted to see and talk to those voices I heard."

Deidre about jumped out of her seat when she heard yelling and realized it was André. André was standing and yelling at Cassie, and boy was she mad. "Will you please shut your stupid, mean-hearted, ugly mouth!"

While Deidre was involved in Ben talking on the tape, she missed the comment that Cassie had made. "Why couldn't he had made us all happy and just die?" She must have said it loud enough for André to hear.

She couldn't allow André to speak like that, so she tried to stop her. "André that will be enough. You need to calm down and sit down."

André wasn't going to let anyone stop her from speaking her mind. "No, I won't shut up, and I won't continue listening to this moron."

Cassie was now standing and yelling back at André. At one point no one could understand what either one of them were saying. They were both yelling at the same time at the top of their lungs. Finally Casey and Cassie's husband grabbed Cassie and took her to a corner of the room. Deidre grabbed André and let her know that under no circumstances was she going to let her continue this argument.

When everything calmed down and everyone was about to take their seats, André got up from her seat and walked over to Mark. "May I talk to you for a moment?" Mark took a big breath and agreed. Once they were in the other room, André told Mark what she thought needed to be done. "She wins. We can't go on like this. You have to get rid of her. I don't even care if she stays in the office at all. She can go back to her hotel room for all I care. I really wanted to carry out Ben's wishes, but I just can't. I think Ben would understand. He knew the kind of person she was."

Mark agreed. They went back to the others, and he walked up to Cassie and Casey. Then the three of them went into the other room. You could hear Cassie yelling in the other room. Suddenly the door flew open. Cassie came storming in and headed straight toward André. All the while she was yelling at her, "Who do you think you are? You are a nobody. Do you hear me? You are a nobody. You're not going to get rid of me that easy. If anyone is going to leave, it's going to be you! Not me! I'm his daughter, and you're nobody."

Deidre was at her feet, but André held her hand up to her grandmother and stared Cassie straight in her eyes as she firmly but calmly spoke to her, "I think it would be a good idea that you sit the rest of the tape out since it upsets you so much." Cassie tried to interrupt but wasn't able to because André held her hand up and continued to talk. "Maybe you could step outside and get some air and maybe call a friend to comfort you." André lifted her eyebrows as if to say, "Do you understand what I'm saying?"

Cassie stood for a moment, just staring at André. Then she turned to Mark and said, "I'll be at my hotel room. Call me when all this nonsense is done and we're ready to get to business and I get to know what I get from that dead old man. It'd better be good for all the hardship I've had to go through today." She looked over at her brother and told him she'd see him later. Then she and her husband left the room.

Daniel leaned in front of Carissa and commented to Deidre and André, "Should we clap or celebrate somehow?"

Casey must have heard him because he turned to Daniel and gave him a disturbing look. Daniel saw him and sat back into his seat. Casey got up and said something to Mark. Then he spoke to his wife, and they both left the room. Mark explained to the others what was happening. "Casey didn't feel comfortable sitting here while his sister was so upset, so he has decided go get her. They will wait outside until the tape is over."

Deidre was so puzzled over what had just happened. What could André know that could make Cassie leave the way she did. She looked over at André and spoke softly so that Casey wouldn't hear, "I take it you're going to tell me all about this along with what happened earlier."

André never cracked a smile, but she assured her grandmother that she would. André was so disappointed that things couldn't have been the way Ben had wanted it to be. She tired. She really tried. She was so fed up with all this. She wished she could just get the videotape and go home. No one appreciated that Ben was pouring his heart out in this tape. Now that both of Ben's children were not present. She wasn't sure why they should continue the tape. He had made the tape mostly for them. Then she decided she wanted to continue the tape so that she could share with the others Ben's last thoughts.

André remembered the day they made the tape. They had made plans on the phone about where they would do the taping and the time they were going to start. André told Ben to make lots of notes to help him so that he wouldn't forget anything he wanted to say and to keep him on track as well.

The day she arrived to tape Ben, she found him all dressed up in jeans and a sport jacket. He was shaved and had his hair slicked back. "Wow, Ben, you sure are all slicked up. You'd think you were going to a wedding." She thought he'd laugh, but he was all straight-faced and serious.

"Well, I thought I should look my best since I'm going to be a movie star." He ran his hand through his hair and brushed his jacket.

André was surprised that there had never been any home movies of him or his family, not even by friends. "Ben, don't you think it would be nice for everyone to see you on this tape just looking like your charming self."

That finally got a smile out of him. "Little much, huh? I know I'd be a lot more comfortable in my regular clothes. I'll go change while you set up over there."

They had decided just to record in his favorite place, the porch. When Ben came back out, he looked more like himself, the person André had come to love like a grandfather. She tried to get him to relax. "Let's just have some fun with this. I'm not going to hold the camera up to my face. That way you can just talk to me. Do you have the notes I told you to write down."

Ben gave her half of a smile. "I don't need any notes. It's all right here ... and here." He motioned to his head and then his heart.

At first Ben was so nervous that they had to start over a few times. André started kidding around with him and making fun of him. He finally started having fun after that, and the taping really started going. Once they were on a roll, it went fairly fast. She couldn't get over his memory. You'd think he had been rehearsing over and over again in his head what he wanted to say, but he assured her that it was just pouring out of him. The taping only took one day, but afterward André went over the tape and edited it. She went back to Ben's house a few days later to show him what she had done. He smiled the whole time he watched the tape. When it was over, he just sat and looked at André as she was taking the tape out of the case.

She became embarrassed when she realized Ben was just staring at her. "What?"

Ben had a soft, loving expression on his face. "You're the granddaughter I never had. To be honest with you, you're the daughter I never had. I hope you don't get this wrong, Missy, but I love you."

André smiled shyly and replied, "I love you the same way."

CHAPTER 9

As they returned back to the tape, Ben was coming back from one of his breaks. His voice was excited as he started talking about the first time he was invited to Deidre's house for dinner.

Deidre's heart skipped a beat as she smiled and looked over at Carissa, and Carissa was looking back at her, smiling just as big. Deidre looked over at André, and she had a smile on her face as she looked at her grandmother. Deidre could tell André was still very upset, so she put her arm around her and pulled her close to hug her. The three of them remembered the day Ben was talking about. It was such a great day.

Deidre remembered the day she invited him. She came to take him to the doctor and to the corner store to pick up some extra things he thought he'd like to have. After their errands they went to have dinner at Maggie's Diner, which was where they always went because that was where Ben liked to go, and Deidre had to admit the food was good.

During their conversation Deidre decided it was as good of a time as any to ask, "Ben, Brad and I would like to invite you to our house for a family dinner. The whole family will be there. Its Brad's and my anniversary. You would make the day complete if you'd come." Deidre was at a complete surprise when Ben accepted.

"Whoa, dinner? I wasn't expecting that." He paused for a moment. "I guess I could come. When is this dinner? You say it's your anniversary? How many years have you guys been married?"

Deidre was tickled pink that Ben wanted to come. She thought for sure he would make up excuses not to come. "It's our fortieth anniversary, and the dinner is next Saturday at five. But I'd like for you to come at about three so that you can get comfortable with being there before everyone starts arriving. Daniel said he could pick you up because he's coming as Cassie's date. Is all that all right with you?"

When Ben didn't answer right away, she thought he was having second thoughts about coming. "I'm not too good at picking out presents. Annie always did that. The only person I ever bought a present for was Annie, and she was easy to buy for."

Deidre reached across the table and put her hand on top of Ben's hand. "Ben, we don't need or want any presents. We just want to share this special day with our family and a few friends. The only present I want from you is your presence at our party, okay?"

Ben smiled and agreed. "Should I wear a bow on my head."

When the day of the party came, Deidre was running around in a whirlwind. She didn't have to worry about food or refreshments because Brad arranged that. He had the entire thing catered so that Deidre could just relax and enjoy the day. But that was impossible for Deidre. She had been cleaning all week and making sure the yard looked perfect. She loved her home and yard. They lived on a small lake with homes spaced far apart from one another. Brad and she took care of their yard themselves instead of having a yard service. Her house wasn't an extremely large house, but it was perfect for entertaining.

André arrived early to help her grandmother with whatever needed to be done only to discover there was nothing left to do. She had brought a large flower arrangement and a framed picture that she had taken of her grandparents on Easter. She had to go looking for her grandparents. She found them out back, standing on the dock, their arms around each other. She smiled as she watched them. They loved each other so much. André hoped that would be the way her marriage would be someday.

Deidre turned at that moment to see her. "Oh, there she is, Grandpa. Right on time."

She climbed the steps to the yard, smiling all the way. "Oh, hon, I told you not to get us anything, but oh, my goodness, those flowers are breathtaking. Thank you so much." As she took the flowers, André handed her the picture. She didn't wrap it. Deidre and Brad fussed over it, and Brad took the flowers and picture in the house to set them in the living room.

Deidre slipped her arm around André's arm, and they walked up to the deck. "I thought you were going to have me help you, Grandma? Just like always, you have everything done. Why did you want me here early?"

Deidre sat down on the glider, and André sat next to her. "There are still a few things to get done, but most of all I thought it would be nice if you were here when Ben arrived since the two of you are so close. I think it'll make him more comfortable." Andre agreed with her grandmother.

Ben waited for a while on the porch for Daniel to pick him up, but he was so anxious that he decided to walk to where the cars were parked and sit on the wooden box. By the time he got there, Daniel was just pulling up. He jumped out to help Ben in and put his walker in the back of the truck. "I hope it won't be too hard for you to get in. I couldn't use my parents' car because they had plans." Ben assured him that he would be fine and that it wasn't too bad. Daniel noticed the package that Ben was carrying. "What's that you have there, Ben? You know you don't have to bring a gift. That's what Carissa told me."

Ben held the package with such tenderness as if it was very fragile. "It's no big deal. It's just something I had around the house and thought they'd like to have it."

The rest of the way, they talked about everything under the sun. Most of it was about Daniel—college, work, Carissa, which Ben had to razz him about. "So what's up with you and our pretty artist? You have any plans for the future with her? You two are sure smitten with each other."

Daniel was easygoing and didn't let much bother him. He knew Ben was just pulling his leg, or at least he hoped so. "No plans. We're both working and going to school, so there's not much time for anything else. We see each other about once or twice a week, and we talk on the phone just about every night. I like her a lot, but that's all. She seems to like me too, but just like me, she has to focus on school right now."

Ben liked Daniel, and he thought the two of them were good for each other, even if they were just dating. "Boy, this is a long ride, isn't it? Do you drive this all the time, or does Carissa come see you?"

Daniel assured Ben he would never have Carissa drive all that way to see him. Then he realized what he had just said. "It's all right for her to drive and see you because you don't drive, but I can't see having her drive to see me when I can drive. Sometimes we meet halfway and have dinner and spend time together."

Once they were off the interstate, Ben asked if it was much farther. Daniel told him they could stop if he needed a break, but Ben said he was fine. He was just curious about how much farther. Daniel assured him it wasn't much farther. "We'll be there in about fifteen more minutes." Ben didn't realize the girls were driving so far to come see him. He didn't understand why they would come so far just for him.

They entered a neighborhood that was very pretty with lots of trees and nice homes. There was a small lake in the center of all the homes that curved a few times. Daniel started slowing down to a stop. "Well, here we are. I've been here once before. It's really nice."

As Daniel was getting out, Carissa came out to meet them. She went straight to Ben's side of the truck and opened his door. "Hi, Ben, how was the ride? Here, let me help you get out. That's quite a step."

Ben handed the package to Carissa as she helped him out. Daniel was waiting with the walker. Once Ben was out of the truck, he reached out for the package, but Carissa offered to carry it. Ben said, "No, that's all right. I can carry it. It's not heavy." As they started walking toward the house, Ben stopped to look at everything. The yard didn't have a single weed in it, and the grass was thick and lush. There were two large trees on each side of the driveway with lots of evergreens lining the property. There was a large variety of flowers along the front of the house with smaller bushes. The house had red brick on it, and there was a large porch on the front of the house. The house even looked bigger with the three-car garage attached. Ben thought about how the house fitted Deidre perfectly.

As Carissa and Daniel were walking into the house, André was walking out to meet Ben.

Ben couldn't help but smile when he saw her. He'd grown to love her so much. "Well, hey there, Missy! Don't you look all dressed up and pretty."

André smiled as she stepped up to him and then walked alongside of him. "You're looking pretty good there yourself, Ben."

As they stepped in the door, Ben stopped once again to take it all in. This was where one of his angels lived. "This sure is a nice house. How long have Deidre and Brad lived here?"

André had to think about that for a moment. "Gee, Ben, I don't know if I remember how long they've lived here. I know I was a little girl when they had this house built. Their other house was in the country, and after the fire, they decided to just sell the property and downsize because all their kids had grown up and moved away. They must have lived here at least fifteen or sixteen years. My mom grew up in the house that burned down."

Ben understood now why Deidre loved the view of the property he had shown her. She had lived in the country herself once. "What caused the fire? Was anyone hurt?"

André didn't know a lot of the details. "No one was home, and it was caused by a gas leak of some kind. It was a big house with lots of land. I remember walking on some trails, and there were some horses. That's all I remember because like I said, I was a little girl."

As they continued to walk through the house, Ben was trying to look at everything. He thought that Annie would have loved to live in a house like this. Then they came into the main area. The kitchen was on one side, and a large living area with a huge fireplace was on the other side. The whole wall in front of them was filled windows that looked out onto the patio, yard, and water. There were two glass sliding doors. "Wow! This is beautiful."

André agreed. "Yeah, isn't it just perfect? I love being here. Grandma and Grandpa have worked for years to get it to look like this. They did most of the work themselves. Now they just work on keeping it up and enjoying it." Before André guided Ben outside to join the other four, she asked if he would like for her to carry the package he had.

Ben shook his head. "No, that's all right. It's not heavy, and I would like to give it to Deidre and Brad before anyone else comes. It's not anything fancy."

The moment the two of them stepped outside, Deidre came up to them all smiles. "Oh, Ben, you have no idea how happy I am that you came."

Brad's voice came right after hers. "We're both very happy you came. Welcome to our home." Deidre hugged him, and Brad shook his hand. Ben hadn't felt such warmth in a long time. He handed the cloth-wrapped gift to Deidre.

"Ben, I told you not to bring anything, that we just wanted you to come."

Ben looked into Deidre's eyes, and with such deep emotion and love, he said, "It's from Annie and me. It means a lot to me that you accept this gift." Deidre looked at André and Brad and then gently opened the gift.

The gift was very old but very beautiful. It was a handmade pillow with beautiful cross-stitch writing and embroidery on it. It read, "Our Forever Love," and the next line said, "Blessed for Forty Years." Tears came to her eyes as she looked up at Ben. "I don't understand, Ben."

Ben smiled with a few tears in his eyes. "Annie made that for our fortieth anniversary, and I thought it would be better to pass it along instead of it just wasting away in my old shack."

Deidre was about to say something when Brad spoke up first. "What a beautiful gift. Thank you so much, Ben. It will always have a special place in our home."

Deidre couldn't speak. She just nodded her head and then hugged Ben. "Thank you, Ben. I love it."

Ben was happy he had arrived early so he could look around some more and get comfortable. Friends from Deidre's church came, and family members started arriving. Ben knew some of them from the time they had come out to his property and had done some work. They made a point to come and visit with him. He sat and watched as everyone was having a great time. There was so much love and laughter.

As he was watching everyone, a young girl came up and sat next to him. "Hi, you're Ben, aren't you? I'm Serena, André's little sister. I'm thirteen. I'll be fourteen in three months. I wanted to bring a friend, but my parents wouldn't let me. I hear you live all alone in the woods. Do you ever get scared living all alone in the woods?" Ben was about to speak when Serena continued her one-way conversation. "I hear you have horses and cows. How many do you have?"

Ben waited a second to see if she was done. He smiled as he spoke to her, "It's nice to meet you, Serena, and no, I'm not afraid to live alone in my house in the woods. As for the horses and cows, they belong to someone else. They use my land to feed and raise them. I use to have horses and cows, even chickens and pigs, but now that I'm old, I can't take care of them. I'm sorry you couldn't bring a friend. But it looks like there are lots of other kids here and things to do. Do you like to fish?"

Serena listened to Ben and realized why André liked him so much. "Yeah, I like to fish. Do you? Will you go down to the dock with me and fish? I'll go get everything, and there's a place to sit down there." She stopped and looked at him and how old and frail he was. "Can you make it down there? I can help you."

Ben wasn't sure he could make it, but he sure wanted to try. "I'm not sure about going down those steps. I haven't been down steps for years, but if you'll help me, I think we just might make it."

Serena jumped up all excited. "I'll go get everything ready and then meet you at the steps. There's a banister you can hold on to besides just me because I'm not too big or strong as you can see."

Ben chuckled. "I'll meet you at the top of the steps." Serena was off and running as Ben slowly got up and started heading for the yard. He stopped and looked at Carissa and Daniel sitting together near a small waterfall. "Don't the two of you fall in and get wet." They stopped talking to each other long enough to look at him and smile. Ben waved and went on.

By the time he reached the steps, Serena was out of breath, waiting and smiling. "Are you ready, Ben? There's some big fish in this lake. I haven't caught one yet, but they're out there. What should I do to help?"

Ben handed her his walker and told her just to stand next to him so he could use her shoulder to brace himself on and use the banister. Right when they started to go down the first step, Ben heard André's voice yelling, "Serena, what in the world do you think you're doing? Ben, you can't make it down those steps! What if you fall?" She took the walker from Serena and reach for Ben.

"We're doing just fine, André! Who do you think you are? You can't just boss Ben around like that. He wants to go fishing with me. Now just leave us alone."

André looked at Ben, frightened. "I don't mean to boss you around. I just don't want you to get hurt." She gave Serena the walker and told her to move and took her place. "At least I'm a little stronger than her. Are you sure you want to do this?"

Ben was serious when he said, "I didn't mean to cause trouble. I really thought we could do it together. It's been years since I've fished, and there are only five or six steps. But if it really upsets you, I'll pass."

André shook her head. "No! You didn't do anything wrong. I would love to help you get down there to fish. I'll fish with you if you want?"

Boy did that cause uproar. "No! We don't need you to fish with us! It's just Ben and me going fishing! You don't even like to fish!"

As André and Ben slowly took each step, Ben suggested it might be best if it was just Serena and him fishing. Once André got Ben down to the dock and got him situated, she turned to Serena. "You can take it from here. Make sure you take good care of him. I'm going to go get him something to drink."

"I already did, and I got us some food and everything we need to fish. See, we don't need you. Now go away and let us fish. Go flirt with that Davis guy you have a crush on."

Ben snickered, and André put her fist up like she would like to hit her just once. Ben assured her they were fine and suggested she go have some fun.

They fished for hours. They caught a few fish but nothing too big. They talked about everything, or at least Serena did. Every once in a while someone would come and check on them. Ben caught himself watching Serena and thinking about how much of a spitfire she was. He liked her. He liked her a lot.

Deidre came down and told them it was about time for them to come join the party for the anniversary toast and some pictures. Daniel and Brad were there to help Ben up the steps. They actually carried him up the steps.

The day was ending way too soon as far as Ben was concerned. Everyone was slowly leaving. Serena came up to Ben and hugged him. "I have to go now, Ben. Can I come visit you in the woods where you live? Are you going to come again someday and see us? Did you have fun fishing today? I did." Then she stopped and looked him in the eyes. "I like you, Ben. Bye." Then she was off without waiting to see if Ben had anything to say. Ben smiled and whispered, "I like you too, spitfire."

It was time for Ben to say his good-byes. Deidre and André took each of Ben's arms and walked him to the truck. Daniel poked fun at

Ben. "Must be nice to have a nice-looking women on each arm." Ben just smiled.

Once he was in the truck, each of the girls kissed him, and Brad shook his hand. The drive home seemed even longer than the ride there. Ben kept running the day over and over in this mind. Daniel broke his thoughts. "Did you have a nice day, Ben?"

Ben looked straight ahead and answered, "You have no idea how wonderful this day has been."

CHAPTER 10

Deidre sat and listen to Ben as he talked about how his friendship with Deidre and her family became closer and how he thought of them more as family rather than friends.

"After the anniversary dinner, I had visitors at least once a week. Sometimes it was twice a week. It would be just one of them at a time, or two would come at once. Brad would come occasionally with Deidre. Spitfire got to come and visit with André on occasion, and Daniel was with Carissa once in a while. Someone was calling me every day, sometimes twice a day. After I realized how far they were driving, I really appreciated their visits even more. I kept telling myself to try to discourage them from coming because of the distance and time, but I just couldn't bring myself to do it. The one thing I made myself do was refrain from calling them. I was afraid if I started calling them, then I would really end up being a nuisance, so I would just wait for someone to call me.

"That brings me to the day Deidre called and said she was going to Centerville to do a dance recital shooting. On her way back, she thought she'd swing by and see me. I always liked it when she came by after a shooting because she would show me the pictures she took. One time she picked me up and took me with her to a baptism shooting. I loved watching her as she worked. Anyway, back to that one day." Ben started getting choked up and asked André to stop the tape.

Deidre knew where he was going with this part of his story. She had just finished a shooting in Centerville for a dance recital. I had gone really well, and she couldn't wait to get to Ben's and go through the pictures with him. She was tired, but it was a good tired because she was so pumped from the shooting. It was raining hard as she was driving on the interstate. She hated driving in rain like that. She had to slam on her brakes once, and her purse fell on the floor upside down. That meant a lot of its contents were probably on the floor now. She was going to just leave it there but decided to at least pick the purse up. As she did, she didn't see the pickup truck coming up fast next to her. The truck lost control, and now it was coming in her lane. It kept coming until it ran her off the road. She was desperately trying to get control of her car, but she couldn't. Plus the truck was still running out of control. She remembered that both her and the truck were going down the hill toward some trees, and the last thing she remembered was her car rolling. She didn't know how many times the car rolled before she became unconscious.

When she regained consciousness again, it took her a long time to figure out what was going on. It seemed like she was in a hole because it was dark and closed in. There was something pressing hard against her chest and face. She could hear voices, but where were they? She couldn't see anyone. Then she slowly realized she was still in her car, but she wasn't sure where. She realized there was a person very close who was yelling at her, but she couldn't quite understand what this person was saying. She knew she needed to call back to this person, but she couldn't. Why couldn't she yell back? The only thing left to do was pray. As she was praying, she lost consciousness again.

Pain brought Deidre back to consciousness. When she opened her eyes, she realized she was in her car, and the car was on its side, her side laying on the ground. Her air bag was lying deflated against the steering wheel. When she looked through her windshield, she saw the truck laying upside down on the front of her car. She heard that voice again, the one she had heard earlier, but this time she understood what it was saying.

"Ma'am, can you hear me? We're working hard to get you out. Can you hear me? Say something to let me know you hear me."

It took everything Deidre had in her to speak, and even then it came out so weak. She hoped the person heard her. "Yes, I hear you."

The person, who Deidre now realized was a man, shouted out to some other people, "She spoke!" Deidre could hear cheering somewhere in the distance. The man asked, "Can you tell me your name?" Once again it took a lot for Deidre to tell him her first name. Then he continued, "Can you tell me if you're hurt?" It was getting harder to speak, so all she could say was yes, and that was very faint. Things started getting hazy again, and Deidre wanted to go back to sleep. The man kept talking to her, but she no longer felt strong enough to answer. Then she heard sirens, lots of sirens. She could no longer stay awake and slipped into unconsciousness again.

Pain once again woke Deidre up, but this time it was excruciating pain. Someone was in the car with her and was speaking to her. "Deidre, can you hear me?" She answered, but her response came out like a groaning sound.

The man in the car with her—she now knew he was a fireman—was explaining what they were doing. "We're getting ready to undo your seatbelt in order try to put you seat back and recline it. Can you tell me where you're hurt?"

"Everywhere," was all she could say. Her mind was becoming clearer now, and so was the pain. She tried to ask some questions. "Is it still raining?" The man said yes. Then he started to ask her a question, but she interrupted, "My camera. Purse. Call husband" The fireman assured her they would get everything and contact her husband, but first they needed to get her out of the car.

Then she remembered the truck and recalled that it was upside down on top of her car. "Person in truck?" The fireman told her they had already gotten him out and the paramedics were assisting him now.

The fireman left, and another man came into the car. "Hi, Deidre, I'm Samuel, and I'm a paramedic. Can you tell me where your worst pain is at?" She wasn't sure, so the paramedic asked her to move each part of her body one by one. Her head, neck, shoulder, and left arm felt the worse pain. That was when she realized there was blood in her hair and down her face. There was a burning sensation in her right leg, but she couldn't feel her left leg at all.

The paramedic explained what they were about to do. "We're going to strap a back brace on you and lift you out of the car. I'm going to tell you now. It's going to be very painful, but we need you to try very hard to stay conscious. Do you understand?"

Deidre grunted; "Uh-huh." The pain was beyond anything she could have ever imagined. The only way she could stay conscious was to start yelling.

They stopped once to check on her. "Deidre, are you able to let us go on?"

She answered, "Yes." The moment she was out of the car, everything got crazy. There were so many people and so many things being done to her. She heard one question after another to the point where she couldn't remember anything that was asked or done to her.

Deidre was so frightened and tired. She vaguely remembered the ride in the ambulance. The paramedic continued to work on her and ask questions. Then when they arrived at the hospital, everything became crazy again. There were bright lights, and a constant noise going on all around her. People were rushing around. There was so many people doing different things to her at the same time. Then there were all the voices, lots of voices. There were people speaking to her and other people talking to one another, and she couldn't make sense of any of it.

Then finally one person put his face close to her and had her focus on just him as he spoke to her. "My name is Dr. Blake. You were in a car accident, and you're now in a hospital. Do you remember any of what happened?"

Deidre wanted to say yes, but for some reason she couldn't speak. It was like her voice was all dried up, so she slowly nodded her head, or at least she thought she nodded her head. The doctor continued talking to her, his face close to hers. "Let's try this. I would like for you to blink your eyes once for yes and twice of no. Can you do that, Deidre?" She blinked once. He smiled. "Great. We now know you can hear and understand us." He repeated his question. "Do you know you're in the hospital and that you were in a car accident?" Deidre blinked once.

After a few more questions, Deidre was able to speak very softly again but was still not able to nod her head. She couldn't speak much, only enough to say one or two words. Dr. Blake told her what they were planning on doing next. "We're about to take you into emergency surgery in a few minutes, but first your husband is here and needs to see that you're okay and that we're taking good care of you."

The doctor's face moved away, and then there was Brad's face. She was never so happy to see him as she was at that moment, and she started crying. It was the first time she had cried during all that had happened.

"Don't cry, hon. I'm right here, and so is most of the family." She gave a small smile and started to compose herself because she didn't want to upset Brad any more than he already seemed to be. He held her hand for as long as he could before they wheeled her away. He kissed her gently on the lips. "Everything's going to be fine. I'll be right here waiting for you. I love you, sweetheart."

In a small whisper, she said, "Love you."

It didn't matter if Deidre was an hour late. It happened on occasion, but she usually called him to let him know she was running late. But Ben was worried now. It was going on three hours late, and still there was no Deidre and no phone call. Ben decided to break his promise to himself not to call and bother anyone.

Deidre had helped him pick out a cell phone, and Carissa taught him the basics on how to use it. André had programmed all the names and numbers in it. Deidre didn't answer her phone. Ben was going to call it again but decided to call Brad instead. There was no answer on his phone. The next number was André's, but just as he was looking for her name and number, there was a knock on the screen door.

"Ben, Ben, where are you? It's me, André. Can I come in?" She never once stopped knocking, and she started calling out to Ben again.

Ben had to hurry to let her know he was there before she broke the screen door in. "I'm here. I'm here. Come on in." The moment he saw her walk in, he knew that it was about Deidre and that it wasn't good.

André walked right up to Ben and grabbed both his hands. "Grandma's been in a car wreck, and it doesn't look good for her. Oh, Ben, she's not good at all."

Ben released her hold on him, grabbed her hand, led her to the small couch, and guided her to sit down. "Now calm down Missy, so you can tell me everything. Please ... I need to know everything."

André took a couple of deep breaths and started getting her composure back. "I don't know all the details, only that she was ran off the interstate by a truck. Her and the truck both went off the side of the road at the same time and went down a steep hill. Her car flipped over, and she ended up on her side. Get this. The truck was upside down and on top of the front of Grandma's car. The guy in the truck was injured, but no way near as much as Grandma. I knew Grandma was coming here to see you, so Grandpa asked me to come by on my way to the hospital to let you know because we knew you'd be worried."

Ben sat there, stunned "What size of truck was it? What hospital is she in? What type of injuries does she have?"

Now it was André's turn to calm Ben down. She put her hands gently on his shoulders. "It's your turn to calm down, Ben, or you won't be able to understand anything I tell you."

Ben relaxed his body a little and nodded in head in agreement with her.

"Grandpa told my mom it was a pickup truck and not a real big one. Mom told me what kind, but I don't remember what she said. As for Grandma, she's in a hospital in Richmond. I don't know what all her injuries are, but she's in emergency surgery right now." André stood to leave. "I'll call you as soon as I know something."

Ben stood up at the same time and started shaking his head. "Oh no, you don't! You're not leaving without me. It'll only take me a couple of minutes to get my pills I'll need, and I'm going with you." He didn't stop for a second to see André's reaction.

"Ben, I have no idea how long I'll be there. It could be all night." That's all she could say before Ben was back and heading for the door.

"It doesn't matter how long. I'm going. Let's get started. The hospital is about forty-five minutes away." The hospital was the same hospital that Annie had been in.

André was going to try to convince him to stay, but he quickly brushed by her and was on his way down the ramp to her car. She shut the door and started walking behind him.

On the drive to the hospital, André tried to fill Ben in with a few more statistics that her mother and grandfather had told her. "They say she can't feel her left side and she has a broken collarbone. Her leg is broken in two places, and her arm and shoulder is broken somewhere. There's something about internal bleeding, so that's why they had to take her into emergency surgery. That's everything I know.

Ben didn't say anything except that they should take the next exit. André was confused. "My GPS says to the exit after this one."

"This way is faster. It takes you right to the emergency entrance. The other way is slower, and it takes you to the main entrance, so you'd have to drive around to the back side."

André didn't argue. She could tell he knew exactly where they were going.

As they entered the hospital, Ben remembered the times he had taken Annie here because of her cancer before she had said she was done with it all. The first person he saw was Serena, and she came running up to him to hug him. André scolded her, "Serena, take it easy. You could have knocked Ben down."

Ben smiled with his eyes. "I think I'm a little stronger than that. Hi, Spitfire, how are you holding up?"

Right at the time, Ben was walking to the place where the family was all gathered. A nurse came and spoke to Brad, Marie, and Taylor. Marie came over to the family to explain what was happening. "Mom's in recovery, and we're going to meet with the doctor to find out the results of the surgery. We'll be right back."

It seemed like hours before they came back, and only Marie and Taylor came. Brad went to be with Deidre. You could tell Marie had been crying, but she was smiling as she started explaining everything to the family. "Mom is stable, but she's not awake yet. They stopped the bleeding and set her collarbone. That's all they did right now. They're going to wait and see how she's doing before they work on her leg and arm. Oh, and her back is fine, so that's another worry out of the way. She'll be in recovery for about an hour, and then they'll put her in intensive care. The earliest that she'll be allowed to have visitors is tomorrow sometime. Dad, Taylor, and I are the only ones who will be allowed to see her today, so everyone might as well go home. I'll keep everyone informed in group text messages."

Everyone was relieved to hear the news, but some were disappointed because they weren't going to get to see Deidre. André came to sit by Ben. "Could you hear everything Mom said from here?"

Ben nodded. "It's great news, but it sounds like she has a long ways to go before she's out of the woods."

André agreed. "I know you don't text, so I'll keep you up on all the news that Mom sends out in her messages. We might as well get you home now."

André stood, but Ben remained seated. "You go ahead. I'm going to stay here."

André tried to talk some sense to Ben. "Ben, there's no reason for you to stay. You can't see Grandma, and you can't stay here by yourself. I promise I'll bring you to see her as soon as the doctor says she can have visitors."

Ben just looked straight ahead and refused to go. "You go on home. I don't need anyone to babysit me. I said I was staying, and I mean I'm staying. Now that's that. Now go on. Go home. I have my phone on me if you want to check on me. Go on, missy. Go home."

André had never seen this side of Ben, but it was obvious that she wasn't going to change his mind. She agreed to leave. "I'll be calling to check on you, and I'm going to let Mom know you're here. If you need to go home, don't think twice about asking Mom or Uncle Taylor to take you. They won't mind. Please tell me you'll at least do that. Do you have some money on you for coffee or something to eat later?"

Ben assured her that he was fine. As André was leaving, he could see she was talking on the phone, probably her mother. She looked back at him one more time and waved. He smiled and waved back.

An hour went by, and Taylor came out and talked to Ben. "Hey, Ben, how are you doing?" Ben assured him he was fine. "Mom woke up for just a few minutes, and now she's resting fine. There's really nothing going on until tomorrow. I'm heading home to get some rest. Why don't I drop you off at your house? Someone can bring you back tomorrow."

Ben smiled and thanked him for the offer. "I'm just fine right here you go get your rest. I just can't bring myself to leave. I would just sit at home all alone, waiting until tomorrow came, so I might as well sit here. No need for you to try to change my mind. I'm old and set in my ways. André will be checking on me, so I'll be just fine."

Taylor checked to see if he could go get him something before he left and if he needed some cash for the vending machines. Ben once again assured him that he was fine.

Another hour passed, and Marie came out. She was surprised to see Ben was still there. "Ben, I thought Taylor took you home." He looked up at her and gave a small smile.

She sat down next to him. "Why didn't you go home when Taylor left? Did you see Taylor when he left?"

Ben explained to her like he did the others. "I saw him, and he offered me a ride home. But I turned it down. I just don't want to be home all alone, waiting and wondering. Here I at least I feel I'm closer to her."

Marie understood what Ben was feeling. "I know. I feel the same way, but it's so late. When was the last time you had something to eat and drink?" She didn't even wait for an answer because she knew he probably didn't have much of anything. "Come on. Let's go get something together. I could use something to eat myself."

Ben didn't argue. He wanted the company as much as he wanted something to drink. The only thing in the cafeteria was the vending machines with sandwiches, chips, fruit cups, and other simple things. Then there was the coffee machine and soda machine. They both had a sandwich and coffee and sat down at a table.

Marie really never had the chance to talk to Ben or really get to know him, but her daughter, André, talked about him all the time. She had come to love him like a grandfather, and her mother, Deidre, loved him just as much.

They talked about Deidre's condition but not that long. They talked about Ben's relationship with Deidre, André, and Carissa. He explained to her about how they were his three angles. Ben didn't want to sound nosy, but there was something on his mind for a long time that evening. "Did someone get Deidre's bag with her camera and stuff in it? I hope nothing happened to it. I know it means a lot to her. You know she was heading to my house when the accident happened. If she has a picture shooting out by my way, she likes to come by afterward and show me the pictures she took. She's so good at it, and she really loves it."

Marie assured Ben that they had Deidra's camera case, purse, and cellphone. "The firemen that helped get her out of the car brought them to the hospital." They talked for a while longer before Marie said she wanted to get back to the room so that she could take a sandwich and coffee to her father. "He won't leave her side, and he won't sleep because he's constantly watching all the monitors that she's hooked up to. I have to leave shortly, so I thought I'd better get him something before I left." Ben could relate to how Brad was feeling.

A couple of hours later, Marie saw Ben before she left the hospital. "Are you sure you don't want me to take you home so that you can at least take a nap? Someone can bring you back later this morning?"

Ben gently shook his head and told her, "No thanks," and then he watched as she went through the revolving doors. He thought to himself; *Now it's only me and Brad waiting for you, sweetheart, to show us that you're fighting for your life. We know you can do it. We're here for you.*

CHAPTER 11

Ben had dosed off, so he was startled when he felt someone touch his shoulder. When he opened his eyes, he was surprised to see Brad ... and also suddenly frightened. "Is everything all right? Things haven't gotten worse, have they? Please tell me she's okay."

Brad calmed him down. "She's doing better. All her vital signs are improving. I knew you were still here, so I thought I'd give you the good news. Besides, I needed to take a walk."

Ben sighed with relief. "Thank you so much, Brad, for coming to tell me. I know you don't want to be away from her for very long, so you coming out here to tell me means a lot to me."

Brad smiled and put his hand on his shoulder. "Why don't I get us both a cup of coffee. I'll be right back." Ben was about to tell him he didn't need to do that, but Brad was already walking away. Ben noticed how tired Brad looked and the strain in his face. He knew how exhausting all this was. He remembered how it was with Annie.

Brad came back with two cups of coffee, but he didn't sit down. "Why don't you come with me and keep me company in the ICU where Deidre is."

Chills ran all through Ben's body. He got up quicker than he had ever gotten up out of a chair in years. He walked faster than he had in a long time, but he still felt it wasn't fast enough.

The ICU unit was brighter and busier than the waiting area. When Ben first saw Deidre, it set him back for a moment. She didn't even look like the Deidre he knew. She was so pale, and there were so many monitors on her. As they walked in, a nurse was in the room, checking on a few things. She turned to see who entered the room. She glanced briefly at Brad but took a long look at Ben. Brad immediately commented. "Nurse

Donna, this is Ben, Deidre's adopted father. He's going to stay with me for a while." Ben nodded at her, and she smiled at him.

The nurse left the room and Brad motioned for Ben to step up to the bed. When Ben stepped up, he just stared at Deidre and slowly stroked the side of her face with the back of his hand. "Can I hold her hand?" Ben was already at his side with a can of disinfectant foam. Ben cleaned his hands and then gently put his hand on top of her hand. He had no idea how long he stood there, just stroking her hand and looking at her.

Brad interrupted his thoughts. "Ben, why don't you come sit down for a while. I promise she won't be going anywhere, and you'll be able to see her from your chair."

Ben sat down and gave a big sigh. "Brad, I'm so sorry that you have to go through all of this. I know how awful it is. I know that knot you have in your stomach and how helpless you feel. But you know how strong Deidre is. She'll pull out of this just fine. You have to believe that."

Brad looked down at his coffee. "That's what I'm depending on. She's a fighter, and she's as stubborn as a mule. I'm hoping she'll give it all she has to recover. I've been talking to her and telling her that she'd better get started on fighting for her life or I'll really be upset with her." He smiled just a little when he said it.

Ben didn't say a word. He felt Brad needed to talk more than listen to advice, so he just sat and listen as Brad continued to talk about Deidre.

"I fell head over heels for that woman the moment we met. Everything just clicked for both of us. We were so young when we met, but we both knew that our love was for real and forever. We've had our share of troubles. But we learned from them, and our marriage and love only became stronger by them. She's a strong-willed woman. Sometimes that's good, and sometimes that's bad. What makes her so special is that she's a good and godly women, and that's what's made our family so close." Brad was quiet for a few moments. "You know, Ben, I was upset with her when she told me the story about how she and the girls met you. That could have been a dangerous situation, and that's not the first time she's put herself in a situation like that. Well, I think maybe that day she met you was probably the scariest story she's told me. Every time she does something that puts her in jeopardy, she promises me she'll try harder to think first before doing something. She really can't help herself. She has such an adventurous spirit.

And those two granddaughters of ours would follow her to the ends of the earth." There was silence again for a few moments. "Deidre told me a little about you and your wife. It sounds like you and I are both pretty lucky to have such loving and devoted wives. Deidre has always been there for me and has supported me in many decisions that I've made. I can't imagine living my life without her. She's a part of me, and I need her to complete my life." Brad's voice cracked. "I think I'll take a small walk. You watch over our girl while I'm gone, okay?"

Ben smiled. "Sure. Take all the time you want. I'm not going anywhere." After Brad left, Ben walked up to the side of the bed and once again took Deidre's hand and just stared at her. "You were there for me when I was about to give up on life, and you have brought life back into my life. I'm here for you, Deidre, and I'm not leaving until you're ready to face this life again on your own. You are so lucky to have a family that loves and needs you. Did you hear what I said? They need you. You're the backbone of your family. You and your family have made me feel like I'm part of your family, and you have no idea how much that means to me."

There was a voice behind him. "Excuse me. Is this Deidre Hugely's room?" Ben turned to answer and was surprised when he saw a woman who looked like a younger version of Deidre. He knew this had to be Deidre's youngest daughter, the one who lived out of town. He didn't know much about her because Deidre didn't talk about her very often. He knew there were problems between the two of them.

Before he could say yes and introduce himself, Brad stepped up behind her, and another man was with him. "Kay, hon, I'm so glad you came." The two of them hugged, and Kay started crying. They spoke for a few minutes, and then Brad did the introductions. "Ben, this is my and Deidre's youngest daughter, Kay, and her husband, Erin. Kay, this is Ben, a very close friend to the family, I guess you'd say we've adopted him." Brad noticed the puzzled look on her face. Brad continued, "It's a long story that I can tell you all about later."

Kay walked up to Ben and reached for his hand. "It's good to meet you, Ben. I'm sorry we had to meet under these conditions." Ben was astounded by how much she was like Deidre. She smiled like her, and her voice was even similar to Deidre's.

Ben shook her hand. "It's good to meet you too. My goodness, you're the spitting image of your mother."

Kay smiled. "I've been told that most of my life."

Ben stepped away from the side of the bed so that Kay and Brad could be with Deidre. "I'm going to go to the waiting room so that all of you can be alone with Deidre." Brad thanked him. Ben had to look one more time at Deidre before he left the room.

Morning finally arrived, and the hospital started buzzing as more and more people arrived. Marie was the first family member to arrive. "Good morning, Ben. Do you need anything before I go see Mom?"

Ben shook his head no. "No, I'm fine. Your sister Kay and her husband are here."

Marie told him she knew about it. "Dad called to let me know she was here and updated me on Mom. I heard you got to spend some time with her. I'm so glad. Now if you need to go home, don't hesitate to tell one of us. We don't mind taking you. Besides, it's not that far from here." Ben let her know he was fine for the time being. "Well, I guess I'd better go see Mom and my sister. I'll see you later."

The next family members to arrive were Taylor and his wife, and the conversation went the same way it had with Marie. Ben was getting the idea that it wasn't just Deidre and Kay who shared a problem. There was also a problem between the children—or so it seemed. Ben thought, *Every family has their problems.* Now he understood why Deidre understood his situation with his children. Deidre had problems of her own with one of her children.

More and more family members arrived. Then Ben saw André and Carissa come through the doors at the same time. They both walked straight over to Ben to check on him. Just as they did, Kay, Erin, and Brad walked into the waiting room. Everyone gathered around them and greeted Kay. Brad updated everyone on Deidre. "She's awake." There were instant tears in Ben's eyes. "Everyone will be able to see her. But it might take a while because they only want two or three visitors at a time, and they said she will need a break between visitors."

Kay talked awhile with some of the family and then walked up to Ben. "Dad told me the story about how you and Mom met. Welcome to the family. I'm glad I was able to meet you, and I hope to see you again." Ben responded with same sentiments.

Brad left with Kay and Erin. Ben was hoping maybe Deidre and Kay were able to make amends or at least start to make amends. André came and sat down next to him. "I'm so surprised to see Aunt Kay here. Did you get a chance to talk to her? Doesn't she look just like Grandma?"

Ben said yes to both questions.

Carissa came and sat on the other side of Ben. She talked across Ben to André. "Wow, were you as surprised as I was to see Aunt Kay here? She looks great, doesn't she? I didn't realize how much I missed her until I saw her. I wish she would start being a part of this family again. Do you think her and Grandma talked for a while?"

André and Carissa commented back and forth for a while before Ben interrupted them, "I was with your grandmother when your aunt Kay arrived. I thought she was very nice and friendly. She looks and even sounds like your grandmother. I hope Deidre and Kay had a nice visit. That would really lift Deidre's spirits at such a difficult time right now."

As the day went by, everyone was able to see Deidre. André walked up to Ben and gave him his walker. "Come on, Ben. It's our turn to go see Grandma, and then you're going home to rest. And there won't be any arguments."

Ben got up and started walking. "We'll see."

Ben was so pleased with the way Deidre looked. She was so alert, and she even smiled. She didn't talk much, but she didn't have to. André talked the whole time. Ben was just happy to sit and watch as Deidre lovingly listened to her granddaughter. After a while Brad came in and told them it was time for Deidre to rest. André kissed her grandmother and said her good-byes. Ben went up to her and kissed her hand. Deidre smiled as she spoke softly to him, "I don't know if it was a dream or if you were here speaking to me, but I remember you saying how lucky I was and that my family needed me." Ben smiled and told her it wasn't a dream. Deidre squeezed his hand and thanked him for being there. "I also remember you saying that I was there for you and that you were going to be here for me." Ben had tears in his eyes now as he assured her that he had said that. He then reach over and kissed her on the cheek and said his good-byes.

On the drive back to Ben's place, both he and André remained quiet. Once they got there, André sat with Ben on his porch for a while before she kissed him good-bye and started heading to her car. She stopped and turned around and was surprised to see that Ben had already gone into the house and the door was closed. She knew he had to be overly exhausted.

After four more days in the ICU, Deidre was ready to be transferred to a hospital in Indianapolis, which was closer to home. Ben was happy for her, but it would mean that he wouldn't be able to see her once they moved her. Daniel and André had been taking him to go see her every day, which now wouldn't happen, but he knew he would be talking to her on the phone every day.

After she had been in the hospital for two weeks, Deidre was excited to go home. There was going to be someone with her at all times, and her activities were going to be very limited. But that was just fine with Deidre as long as she was going to be in her own home.

Brad was so happy to take his wife home after all she'd been through. He missed her being home with him. As they were riding home, they talked and laughed. "I might as well tell you now before you see all the cars. There's a homecoming party waiting for you at home. One thing you need to know ahead of time is no one's going to let you overdo it. It's going to be a small and short party, but there was no way of stopping our family from wanting to all be there when you got home." They went around the turn in their neighborhood, and then she saw all the cars and a large rental sign saying, "Welcome Home." Tears came to Deidre's eyes as Brad placed his hand on hers and said, "Welcome home, sweetheart."

Everyone was in the yard, yelling, "Welcome home," as they pulled in their driveway. Marie ran up to the car to open the door, and Taylor was right beside her with a wheelchair for Deidre. There were tears, hugs, and laughter all the way to the front door. The last person Deidre saw was Ben standing close to the door, waiting for her. "Oh, Ben, I'm so glad you came. I've missed you. I got used to seeing you every day while I was in Richmond. Once I came to Indy, I missed your visits. They meant a lot to me."

As Deidre was wheeled into her house, she looked around and then closed her eyes and took a big breath. "It is so good to be home." Then she was wheeled into the family room, where there was a large sign draped above the fireplace that said, "Welcome Home."

The party was short just as Brad had said. Just before everyone was about to leave, Carissa got everyone's attention by tapping the side of her glass. "Hey, everyone, I have something to announce." Once she got everyone's attention, she continued to speak. "Next month there is an art showing at school, and a few of my pictures were picked to be on display." Everyone was cheering and congratulating her. She quieted everyone down so that she could continue. "I would love for everyone to come, but you'll need a ticket. They're free. I just need to know who's all coming so that I can get the tickets."

Everyone surrounded Carissa as she quickly wrote down the names of everyone who wanted a ticket. André wheeled Deidre over to where Ben was sitting. They talked awhile about Carissa's news. After a few minutes, Carissa walked over to the three of them. "Ben, I hope you don't mind that I put your name on the list. It would mean a lot to me if you would come. I already talked to Daniel about bringing you. Please say yes."

Ben was thrilled that Carissa felt that way. "Well, since my name is already on the list, I guess that means I'll be there." In a more serious tone, Ben continued, "I would love to come. I wouldn't miss it for the world." Then he looked over at Deidre. "Are you going to be well enough by then to go?"

Deidre smiled at Ben and then at Carissa. "Like Ben said, I wouldn't miss it for the world."

Everyone started leaving right after Carissa's news. Ben was waiting on Daniel, so he was one of the last to leave. He was glad he was able to stay for a while longer. Brad had situated Deidre in a recliner in the family room. There was a table next to the chair, and Brad put a snack tray on the other side. He brought her a blanket and some water. André brought her the remote to the television and Deidre's cell phone. Ben could tell Deidre was in good hands. Deidre looked over at Ben. "Boy, I could get used to this."

Then André walked up to Deidre. "Grandma, here's an envelope with the pictures that you had taken at the recital before the wreck. I developed them, and I found the paperwork that you had on the client, so I called them and met with them. I explained to them what had happened to you and told them I wasn't sure which pictures you were planning on showing them, so I took all of them. They pick all of them except three. That made it fifty-two pictures they wanted. I found your price list on your desk. I hope that's the current prices. So it's all done and paid for."

It took a moment for Deidre to understand everything André was explaining to her. She was so amazed by what she was saying. "You did all that? They bought fifty-two prints? André, that's amazing. I'm so proud of you. Maybe I should have you do all my presentations for me. I don't know what to say except thank you. I knew it was a great shoot, but to have them buy that many prints— I don't think I could have done that good of a job myself. Thank you so much, sweetheart. You have no idea how much that means to me."

Carissa came back into the room to tell Ben that Daniel was ready to go. Ben hated to leave but he knew Deidre needed to rest. As Daniel and Ben were leaving, Ben felt a relief that he hadn't felt since the wreck. Deidre was home and in good hands.

CHAPTER 12

There were days that flew by and days that seemed to just creep by for Ben. André came to see him about once a week, and Carissa came by a couple of times. Ben talked to Deidre a couple of times a week, but he really missed seeing her. One day Daniel came by to drop off groceries and do some yard work for Ben. Ben always sat on the porch while Daniel worked. "Hey, Ben, I'm going to go see Carissa tomorrow. Deidre asked if I could bring you by to see her. Would you like to go?"

Ben's heart skipped a beat. "That would be great. Deidre didn't mention it to me yesterday when I spoke to her. Are you sure it's okay with her?"

Daniel assured him it was all right.

When Daniel picked Ben up, he had brought a bouquet of flowers with him. After he helped Ben in the truck, he handed the bouquet to him. "My mom said you called her and wanted her to put a bouquet together. She hopes you like what she did." Ben told him they were beautiful and asked him how much he owed. "Mom said to not worry about it. She just hopes you and Deidre like them. She also wanted you to tell Deidre that she's thinking about her and praying for her every day." Ben told him he would call Sara later to thank her for the flowers and the prayers.

Ben was so pleased to see that Deidre looked like her old self again. She had even made dinner for her, Brad, and him. As he handed her the flowers, he felt like he should be helping her. "I had Sara put these flowers together for you. She wanted me to let you know she's thinking and praying for you. Should you be doing all this? Is there anything I can do to help?"

As Deidre thanked Ben for the flowers, she continued to explain her progress to him. "I'm just fine. All I'm really doing is making up a salad, and I'll warm up some bread. There's a casserole in the oven that a neighbor brought over yesterday. I do things in small doses like make the bed and then rest or dust a couple of rooms and then rest. I worked out in the yard a couple of times but could only do a little at a time, and Brad wouldn't let me do that unless he was home and outside with me." She was finished with the salad and came over to sit with Ben. Deidre was still using a cane to walk.

The evening went by so quickly. Before Ben knew it, Daniel was there to pick him up. Carissa came to see him for a few minutes before they left. Just before Daniel and Ben drove off, Carissa came over to Ben's side of the truck. "Don't forget that the showing is in ten days. I'll see you then." She reached up and kissed him on the cheek. He patted her on her cheek and said he couldn't wait.

André called Ben a couple of days later and made plans to take him shopping for a suit to wear to the showing. When she showed up, Ben wasn't sure he wanted to go. "I have an old suit. All it needs is to be taken to the cleaners."

André asked to see it, and Ben brought it to her. It was old and dusty. She swiped the dust off the shoulders and tried to look it over. "Ben, why don't you try this on for me? Let's see how it fits. It looks a little big." Ben grumbled but did as she asked. When he came back in, André couldn't help but snicker. "You must have lost a lot of weight since you wore that last."

Ben knew she was right. "It was a little big on me when I wore it to Annie's funeral. Now it looks like it's even bigger, so I guess that means we'd better go buy me a suit. If nothing else, I can wear the new suit to my own funeral."

André gave Ben a displeased look. "I hate it when you talk like that."

Ben didn't know it upset her that much. "I'm sorry, Missy. It's just when you get as old as me, you except death because you know it's not that far off. It's all part of living. Now let me go get changed, and we can go get me some fancy clothes."

As he turned and started to walk to his bedroom, André decided to tell him a secret. "You might have some place else to wear the suit we're going to buy today." Ben stopped to look at André with a puzzled face. André knew she shouldn't say anything, but she just couldn't help herself. She was busting at the seams to tell someone. "Daniel and Carissa are engaged!"

Ben's mouth fell open. "They're going to announce it at dinner before the opening. Oh, by the way, Carissa asked me to invite you to the dinner."

Ben was shocked. They had only been dating for a few months, and Daniel had said their education had to come first. "What in the world? They don't even know each other that well. What about their educations?"

André was set back by Ben's reactions. She thought he would be happy for them. "They're not getting married for about a year. They've been talking about everything, and they're still going to go to college. Between now and the date they set for the wedding, which will be announced later, they're going to double up on classes and take summer classes. Aren't you happy for them, Ben?"

Ben should had known that they both would be sensible about their plans for the future, and he thought from day one that they were perfect for each other. "Oh, I'm happy for them. I just needed to know they weren't jumping into this too quickly and were still thinking about their educations. I think they're great for each other. Now I'd better get changed so we can get going."

Ben wasn't that picky about what suit to buy, but André was very picky right down to the tie and shoes. "Shoes? Why do I have to buy shoes? I have some brown dress shoes at home."

André shook her head. "We bought a dark blue suit, so you can't wear brown shoes with a blue suit. Oh, and we need to get you some dark blue socks."

Now Ben was really confused. "Socks? Who's going to look at my socks?" André didn't even respond. She just gave Ben a look that said, "Enough is enough." Ben had to admit to himself that he was enjoying the time with André and the fuss she was making over him.

* * *

Ben was very anxious as he was waiting for Daniel to come pick him up for dinner and the art show. He hoped he wouldn't let it slip that he knew about he and Carissa being engaged. He also hoped Daniel didn't forget the bouquet of flowers that he had asked Sara to put together for Carissa.

He heard a car and knew it was Daniel, so he started getting up from his chair on the front porch. He was surprised when he saw Sara walking up to the house. She was carrying a box. When she saw Ben, she stopped and stared at him. Ben could see tears forming in her eyes. "Oh, Ben! You look so nice. Annie would have loved how nice you look."

Feelings rushed through Ben as he thought about Annie. "Why are you here, Sara? Is something wrong with Daniel?"

Sara started walking again. "No, he's in the car. John and I were invited to dinner and the art show. I thought I'd bring you a casserole, chicken, and a few other things I made. There's a pie in here too. I'll take it to the kitchen. You can wait for me, or you can start heading for the car." Ben thanked her for the food. "I might as well start heading for the car since it takes me a while to get there." While she was in the house, Sara decided to grab Ben's wheelchair since she knew they would be doing a lot of walking.

The ride was quiet except for a little small talk. Ben was afraid to say too much in fear that he would spill the beans that he knew about the engagement. But the silence was too much. "Well, it's nice that you and John could come. Daniel, are you as proud of our little artist as I am?"

"She's amazing. Did you hear that next semester she's taking both graphic art and designer art classes? I hope it won't be too much for her, but she assured me she'll make it through okay. She wants to double up her classes so that—" Daniel stopped in the middle of his sentence. Sara questioned him about why she wanted to double up her classes. Daniel gave a lame answer. "So that she can get them out of her way and be evaluated on what direction is best for her." Sara asked a few more questions but seemed to get more confused with each answer Daniel gave.

Ben snickered quietly to himself. Daniel gave him a questionable look. Ben decided to help Daniel out. "I don't understand all that college or art stuff. We'll just have to trust that Carissa knows what she's doing." Sara agreed, and everyone became quiet again.

When they arrived in downtown Indianapolis, John asked Sara to help him find a parking place or a parking garage not too far from the restaurant where they were going to have dinner. Once they parked, Ben was glad Sara had grabbed his wheelchair. He probably could have walked to the restaurant; however, Daniel said they were going to walk to the convention center after dinner, and that was quite a ways away.

Ben had never been to a restaurant as nice as this one, so he was trying to take it all in and at the same time greet people as they came up to him. Everyone went on and on about how nice Ben looked. He told them about the shopping experience he had with André, and they all laughed.

Serena popped up in front of him and hugged him. "Hi, Ben, can I sit next to you?" Ben smiled and told her sure. André argued with Serena, "Did you ever think that maybe other people would like to sit next to him."

Serena put her hand on her hip in a sassy way. "Well, he has two sides."

Ben had to laugh at the two of them. They were such typical sisters. "I have to agree with Spitfire. I have two sides."

Ben loved watching and listening to everyone during dinner. There was so much excitement in the air, and he couldn't stop watching Daniel and Carissa. A couple of times Carissa would look over at him and smile.

Once they started on their deserts, Daniel stood. "May I have everyone's attention for just a moment?" Once he got their attention, he reached his hand out to Carissa, and she stood up next to him. "I would like to tell Carissa that we are all very proud of her." Everyone voiced their agreement. "And I would like to share with everyone that I have asked Carissa to marry me."

Carissa spoke up immediately. "And I said yes!" Everyone stood, clapped, and gathered around to congratulate them.

Ben couldn't get to them, so he just waited until everyone was seated once again. "I couldn't get to you to congratulate the both of you. But I'd like to make a toast to the two of you—if you don't mind—and Brad and you too, John." Both men nodded their approval. Everyone raised a glass, and Ben continued, "My Annie and I were a lot younger than you two, but we knew from the day we met that we were meant to be. Our love was very special. When Deidre was in intensive care, Brad shared with me that his and Deidre's love was the same way. So we—Brad and I and John too—wish the two of you the love we were so blessed to have. May your love be special. To Daniel and Carissa!"

Everyone repeated, "To Daniel and Carissa."

Shortly after the toast, it was time to leave for the art show. Ben couldn't remember the last time he was in downtown Indy, but he knew it had changed a lot. It was no longer a small town, and it was so busy. He wished he could do a little sightseeing, but there just wasn't enough time for that today. A few people drove to the convention center, so a lot of them piled into those few cars. It was crowded, but it was a whole lot better than walking. He'd never seen the convention center before or any of the buildings around it. When he got out of the car, he stood and looked around as everyone else was getting out of the car. With his wheelchair in tow, Deidre came up from behind Ben, but he didn't hear her. "Ben, are you all right?"

"Oh, I'm sorry. I just can't get over how big this city is. It's just not the same place I remembered. There's so many buildings and some really big ones." Ben asked what a few of the buildings were, and Deidre explained.

Deidre stood looking around with Ben. "Why don't we make plans for a day trip here, and I'll drive you all around and show you all of downtown. We can also have lunch down here." Ben loved the idea and started looking around again. Deidre touched his arm. "We need to go now Ben." She motioned to his wheelchair.

Brad pushed Ben into the convention center, but the moment they arrived in the rooms where the art show was being held, Carissa came up and asked if she could push Ben into the showing. Ben noticed that the rest of the group wasn't there yet. "Where's everyone else? Should we wait for them?"

Carissa bent down in front of Ben. "I'm so happy that you came into my life. Because of you, I met Daniel. You're a very special part of this night. I would be honored if I could escort you through the art show."

Ben didn't know what to say. He wasn't sure what she was trying to say. He didn't do anything to deserve this special attention. He looked around and noticed that everyone else had already left. "Sure, hon. Besides, there's no one else to push me. They all left."

Carissa laughed and started pushing him in. She showed him some of the other photos that had won prizes in different categories. She explained to him what it all meant. "There are different types and levels of prizes. There's first-, second-, and third-place prizes in different divisions. Divisions signal experience in years. Sometimes you may be new, but if your prints are really good, you can jump into the next division." She pointed out some of the really good prints and explained why they were so good.

Ben was really enjoying looking at everything, especially since Carissa was showing him and explaining everything. Every once in a while, they would run into a family member and talk for a minute, and then they were off looking again.

"Okay, Ben, my pictures are next. I was so happy when they picked four of my prints. I thought there were only going to be three." When she wheeled him around a corner, everyone was standing there, and they started clapping. Ben thought they were clapping for Carissa, but he noticed they were looking at both her and him. Then he saw the prints.

All Ben could do was stare at the photos. He was shocked and confused. The largest print showed him sitting in his rocking chair on his front porch. It had a first-prize ribbon on it. Then he noticed a smaller print of Annie's place with the sunlight shining through the trees on her stone. She had taken it before they had cleaned it up. It had a second-place ribbon on it. He just kept staring back and forth at the two prints.

Carissa bent down next to him. "What do you think, Ben? You and Annie won first and second prize. It's second division, but I can't believe I won anything. It's all because of you, Ben, you and Annie."

Ben couldn't speak at first. He just kept looking at the prints and shaking his head. Everyone stopped clapping and became quiet. Carissa was concerned about his reaction. "Don't you like them, Ben?"

Ben finally could speak. "Why would a picture of an old man in a rocking chair win first prize?" Everyone started laughing, and Carissa hugged him and started explaining to him about what the judges saw in the print.

After a few minutes, Ben looked at the other two prints. One was of the church that he and Annie had been married in. It was so sad to see it empty and overgrown. He asked Carissa if she knew about the church. "Did I tell you that Annie and I were married in that church?" Carissa told him no. Then he saw a print of a graveyard far away with a large tree next to it. He was puzzled about something. "Don't get me wrong. These pictures are fantastic, but why are all your pictures of old or dead things?"

Carissa laughed as she explained she was going for things with a certain lighting or depth. Ben had no idea what she was talking about, so all he said was, "Oh."

As everyone was looking at the prints, two gentlemen and a lady walked up to the booth and introduced themselves as three of the judges. One of the gentlemen asked if one of them was the artist of the prints. Carissa was about to speak up, but Serena beat her to it. "She is, and this is the man in that picture." She pointed to Carissa and then to Ben. Marie put her hands on her daughter's shoulders and gently pulled her back a ways and whispered in her ear.

The judges congratulated Carissa and asked her questions about the picture of Ben. The lady judge walked up to Ben, reached out her hand to him, and personally introduced herself to him. "I'm Dora Comings. It's a pleasure to meet you." She paused while Ben said his name. She repeated his name back to him. "Ben Crawford, we don't usually get to meet the subject of a picture. I must say you look quite different tonight than in the picture." Everyone laughed.

"Well, the day this was taken is the first day I met Carissa, the artist, and I wasn't expecting any company. It's a long story but a good one." Ben would have loved to tell her the story, but he knew there wasn't time for that. Besides, this night was about Carissa's talent, not how they had met.

Dora asked one of the other judges to go get the cameraman. Then she turned to Carissa and Ben. "I would love to have a few pictures of you and Ben next to the print if you don't mind. And Carissa, if you could write a short story about this picture, that would make it even better."

Carissa agreed and said that wouldn't be a problem.

Ben wanted the judge to know more. "The picture of that gravestone with the sunlight beaming through the trees is a picture of my Annie's place." He hesitated and then added, "My Annie's grave site. It was taken before it was cleaned up … and before the picture of me was taken. That there picture of the old abandoned church is where Annie and I were married. But Carissa didn't know that at the time she took the picture."

Dora stepped closer to the prints and then asked, "Carissa, do you mind if we take these prints down and let Ben hold them for a picture. I love how you caught the light. You'll have to explain how and why you took these pictures. I'm starting to think that this is going to be a very interesting story."

The cameraman came, and they took several different pictures. Ben was smiling from ear to ear. He was going to stand, but they told him it was fine for him to sit in his wheelchair. Dora was so excited about the pictures. With the last picture, she smiled and commented, "I think that might be the perfect picture."

CHAPTER 13

While listening to Ben on the video, André sensed something. When she turned around, she saw Cassie and Casey sitting behind her. She had no idea how long they had been there because she was so engrossed in listening to Ben. When she looked at them, Cassie glanced at André, but it was just for a moment. Then she turned her attention back to the video. André was about to nudge her grandmother to show her that they were there but then decided not to. It was obvious that Cassie and Casey didn't want everyone to know they were watching. Besides, she didn't want to interrupt her grandmother listening to Ben. André knew the tape was getting closer to the end. She was so glad that the twins came back in because Ben had a personal message for them once he got to the end of the tape. André brought her attention back to Ben on the tape.

Once again Ben took a break, but they didn't take a break in the law office. By now everyone wanted to get to the end of the tape.

Ben was sitting down in front of the camera once again. "Okay, where was I?" You could hear André in the background telling him the last thing he had talked about. "Oh yeah, that was my most favorite evening." Ben continued telling about some other visits, and then he got into the holidays. "Boy, oh boy, I've never seen a Christmas Eve celebration like the one at Deidre's house. There were so many people and some really great food. They gathered around and sang Christmas carols, and then Santa Claus came and handed out presents to all the children and even a few adults. There was so much laughter and excitement. I spent the night at Deidre's house on Christmas Eve, and the next morning was the complete opposite of the night before. Christmas morning was quiet and relaxing. Only Brad, Deidre, André, and I stayed over. After a while Brad started fixing this big Christmas breakfast. Deidre invited me to go with them later in the day to a homeless shelter where they helped serve food and hand out presents. I wasn't sure what I could do, but I thought it would be nice so I said yes. It was such an eye-opening experience for me. The people who came were so happy to be there, and they were so thankful for the food and gifts. There was a group of carolers that sang and got the people to sing along. Even if it was only for one day, you could see happiness in those people's eyes."

Deidre remembered how she loved watching Ben that day at the shelter. He asked so many questions. "Where do all these people come from?"

Deidre came up and sat next to Ben for a while and explained to him about the people who were there. "Some live in shelters, some in their cars. Others live in homes but don't have enough money for food and gifts. Then there are some people who actually live on the streets in alleys and under bridges."

Ben was shocked. "None of the people with children live in the streets, cars, or under bridges, do they?"

Deidre sadly said, "Matter of fact ... yes, there are children who live with parents or a parent on the streets." After a few more questions, Deidre had to excuse herself so that she could help out in the kitchen to clean.

On the video Ben was talking about the cold and snowy winter. "I thought once it turned cold and especially when the snow started falling, I would probably not see any of my angels for a while, but that wasn't the case at all. They continued their visits just like normal. There was one snowstorm that hit us hard. I covered most everything on my porch, but there were piles of snow on top of the covers. So I was stuck inside, which really made it tough and more lonely. Next thing I knew John and Daniel showed up with a plow on their truck, and Brad, Deidre, and Carissa came with shovels and food. I had talked to Deidre early that morning and told her about the snow on the porch. I also told her I was fine otherwise, but I guess she had to see for herself. It didn't take them any time at all to clean a path to my house. They cleaned all of the snow off my porch—and I mean all the snow—and uncovered some of the things on the porch. They know how much my porch means to me. Even when it's the coldest day ever, I still come out on the porch on and off all day and sit for a while. Deidre had brought food for everyone to eat that day. It was nice to have company over to visit and eat with them. John and Daniel left right after they ate, and Carissa left with them; however, Deidre and Brad stayed for a while longer. Brad and I watched TV and talked while Deidre did a little cleaning and put away the groceries that she had brought. What I thought was going to be a long and lonely day ended up being a great day."

When Ben got to the part about spring coming, Deidre knew the tape was getting close to the end. Shortly before spring had arrived, Ben started getting tired easily. He just passed it off at first as getting lazy through the winter. Then one day when André called him, he asked her if she might be able to take him to the doctor.

Naturally that freighted André. "Are you okay, Ben? Does this have to do with how tired you've been lately? Have you made an appointment yet with the doctor?"

Ben waited until André was finished with all her questions. "Yes, I'm okay, and yes, it's because I can't seem to shake being tired a lot. And yes, I called and made a doctor's appointment. I was going to call you shortly and ask if you could take me. The appointment is tomorrow at two thirty." André told Ben that wouldn't be a problem.

As André was listening to Ben on the video, she remembered how worried she was that day. She got to Ben's way earlier than she needed to be. The two of them went to lunch close to the doctor's office. Ben tried to ease André's mind during lunch. "You know I probably just have an iron deficiency or something simple like that because I feel fine except for being tired."

André looked at his food and then at him. "And a lack of appetite I see."

Ben lied to her. "I ate not too long ago. But when you said we should go out for lunch, I couldn't turn down an offer like that."

It felt like hours that André had been waiting while Ben was in with the doctor. When Ben came out, the doctor came with him. He started explaining to André what he had told Ben in the examining room. "I'm going to run a complete blood count on Ben, and then he'll need to go to the hospital and get a few tests done."

The doctor continued explaining to André what kind of test they were going to run, but André couldn't take it all in. She just wanted to know if he was okay. "What are you looking for, doctor?"

The doctor was very vague about everything. "I can't be sure right now, so we're going to look into a few things that might be the problem."

André wanted to make sure the doctor knew as much as possible. "Did Ben tell you that he's lost his appetite?"

To André's surprise, the doctor answered, "Yes."

As soon as André was on the road after she dropped Ben off at his house, she called her grandmother. "Grandma, something's wrong with Ben. I took him to the doctor today because of his tiredness, and he's lost his appetite. And he lied to me about it. The doctor's having a complete blood count done, and he wants Ben to go to the hospital to have tests done." When Deidre asked what kind of tests, André couldn't tell her. "I don't remember what kind because I was so upset that I wasn't really listening. I need you to talk over all this. I'm afraid I might mess everything up and miss something important."

Deidre was concerned about how upset André was, especially since she was driving and talking on the phone at the same time. "Don't worry, sweetheart. I'll take over from here. I'll call Ben and get all the information from him. You just calm down, okay?"

"No, Grandma, you're going to have to call his doctor and talk to him because I'm afraid Ben won't be honest with you. He lied to me about his appetite when I questioned him about it, but he told the truth to the doctor. I have the name and the number of his doctor." Deidre agreed to call the doctor but not until she talked to Ben first. André didn't understand. "Why do you have to talk to Ben first? Why can't you just call his doctor?"

Deidre tried to explain everything to André. "I can't just pry into Ben's private life without speaking to him first. He's a grown man, and we're just his friends. I need to have his permission to talk to his doctor. Besides, doctors won't tell anyone about their patients unless they have permission from the patient. So calm down. I'll find out everything, and we'll go from there. Do you understand everything I'm telling you?"

André was quiet for a moment and then answered her grandmother. "Yeah, I understand, but don't let Ben talk you out of talking to his doctor. He really needs those test done." Deidre assured her she would make sure Ben got everything done that needed to be done.

At the law office, André slipped her arm around her grandmother's arm as they continued to listen to Ben talk about the spring, but both of their minds were on what his health was like then.

Deidre waited until the next day to call Ben to get all the details. Ben explained everything that he and the doctor had talked about. "I told the doctor how tired I was and how I seemed to be so weak lately. He checked my lymph nodes and said they were swollen. I told him I was having night sweats and that I felt more pain in my joints than normal. So he ordered a complete blood count to be done. Sara's going to be here in about twenty minutes to take me."

Deidre was glad that Ben was being honest with her. "When do you want to set up the appointments for the tests? Or is your doctor's office going to do that for you?"

Ben explained what the doctor had told him. "After the blood work comes back, the office will notify me. Then they will set up appointments for the tests. So for right now it's just a wait-and-see game."

André called Deidre every day, wanting to know if she had heard from Ben. Deidre was about to call André when the phone rang. "Grandma, have you heard anything yet? It's been four days."

Deidre told her, "Yes, the doctor's office called Ben this morning. We're going this afternoon to see the doctor."

André was happy the doctor called, but she was confused. "I don't understand. Why does he have to see the doctor again? Why can't the doctor just set up the test? Do you like how this sounds, Grandma? I don't."

Deidre had to agree with André. "No, I don't like the way it sounds, but let's not jump to conclusions, okay? I'll call you the moment I get a chance."

André wished she could go with them; however, she had a test at school, and she now had an evening job developing pictures at a camera shop. "You promise to call as soon as you can?"

Deidre assured her once again that she would.

Instead of taking Ben out to lunch, she decided to bring him lunch. She thought a light lunch might make Ben eat better, but he didn't eat hardly anything. She knew there was no use in saying anything, at least not at this time.

Instead of going to an examining room, the nurse led them to the doctor's office. Deidre was glad they didn't have to wait long. Dr. Evans came in carrying what Deidre suspected was Ben's medical files. He greeted them and then sat down on the other side of his desk and opened the file. Ben didn't wait for the doctor to speak first. "Well, doc, what's the verdict? Do I live or die?" Deidre wasn't a bit happy with Ben's comment.

Dr. Evans sat back in his chair and clasped his hands together. "Ben, it doesn't look good." He paused for a minute to make sure he had Ben's complete attention. He continued to talk about what they had found from the blood tests. "You have an acute myeloid leukemia, and it's spreading fast. I need you to go to the hospital and have a few tests done. You'll need a spinal tap, a chest X-ray, and a cytogenetic done."

Ben didn't react quite the way Deidre thought a person should act when he was hearing that he had leukemia. She felt she was more upset than he was—unless he was really good at hiding this emotion. Dr. Evans told him that the nurse had his tests scheduled and that she would go over them with him on their way out.

On the way home, Deidre didn't know what to say, so she decided to wait for Ben to speak first. He was quiet for a long time. "When you take me home, can you stay for a while? I really need to talk to you."

"I can stay for as long as you need me to, Ben." Deidre was thinking about having him come home with her so that he wouldn't be home alone.

Once Ben was situated in his rocking chair on the porch, Deidre went inside to get them some of the ice tea that Sara had brought over the day before. As they both sat on the porch, Ben talked about the history of the land and house. Deidre had already heard the story before, but she let him continue telling her again. After a while he stopped and gave a small chuckle. "I know I've told you all this before, but I just felt a need to talk about it again. After me, there's no one else who's going to continue to keep this land, so I decided to sell some of the land. I just don't want to leave it up to someone else. A few weeks ago, I contacted the people who rent the portion of property that is being farmed and the person with animals who rents the other portion of the land. I've planned on meeting each of them next week in my lawyer's office. After the news today, I guess it's none too soon. I was going to have Sara or Daniel take me, but I would really like it if you would go with me and sit with me during all of it."

Deidre asked when the meetings were scheduled because she had a shoot the next week. When Ben told her the days and times, she said she could. One of the times conflicted with the shoot, but she figured she could reschedule it since it was not live. After a moment Ben started talking again. "Deidre, I need to tell you up-front that if I have to do chemo or radiation or if I see that any treatments is going to just prolong my life for a short time and going to make me sick those last days of my life, I won't do it. I've been ready for a long time to go and be with my Annie. You and your family have been a blessing to me, but nothing replaces the chance to be with my Annie again. I hope you understand what I'm trying to say. I'm done fighting, and I'm done with this life. I'm ready to move on to the next life, which I hear is pretty nice."

What could Deidre say after that? She could argue with him, but it would just sound selfish. All she could say was, "I understand, Ben, but let's just see what's up first."

CHAPTER 14

The story Ben was telling on the video didn't cover even a small portion of what was going on in his life at that time. He didn't mention selling the land or the talk he had with Deidre. The next two weeks were so busy. Deidre had André take Ben to the hospital for all of his tests, and Deidre took him to the lawyer's office both times to sell his land. She could tell that the visit to the hospital for tests and the two trips to the lawyer's office were really taking a toll on Ben. Deidre suggested lunch one day at Maggie's Diner after they went to the lawyer's office, but Ben said he was exhausted. "This week has been so busy that I think I'd rather go home and rest if you don't mind." Deidre assured him that wasn't a problem. When she took him home, she noticed he wasn't getting around very well lately.

Between Deidre, André, Carissa, and the Matthews, there was someone at Ben's house every day. One day when André came over, Ben asked her to take him to the lawyer's office. They were there for about an hour. When they got back, Ben asked André not to tell anyone about their trip to the lawyer's office and then asked if she could take some notes down. That's when André suggested recording everything.

In the lawyer's office, Ben took another break, and when he came back, you could tell he was tired and more serious this time. There was no smile or twinkle in his eye. André took her grandmother's hand and squeezed it. When Deidre looked over at her, she saw tears welling up in her eyes. She knew that André knew what was coming.

"Well, I guess it's about time to end this here movie. This is the hard part. I've heard from the doctors, and it's not good. The leukemia is aggressive. I've decided not to do the chemo and just let God take over from here. So I don't know if it's going to be a week or a few months before

101

I get to leave here and join my Annie. But before I do, I need to say some things that are really heavy on my heart and mind." Ben was quiet for a few minutes, and then when he looked up at the camera, he had tears in his eyes. "I always thought that if you provide a home, food, and clothing for your kids, then that makes you a good father. After knowing Deidre and her family, I realize it takes way more than that. It takes time and giving of yourself to them. It means listening and understanding their needs. It was hard for me to realize that I wasn't a good father. I didn't even know what it meant to be a good father. I just did things the way they were done as I grew up. That wasn't fair to you two and especially to my Annie. All I can say is that I'm sorry, Cassie and Casey, and I know it's too late to do anything about it now. You both deserved so much more. I was lucky that before Annie died, I was able to make it up to her a little. But still, it was not enough for what she went through all those years. I know I never said this to your faces, but I love you both. I'm not asking for forgiveness because I don't deserve it. I miss you both."

The tape came to a stop. That's when everyone realized that Casey and Cassie were in the office because they heard Cassie crying. André and a few others were quietly weeping as well. André's heart went out to Cassie and Casey—at least for a few minutes. Cassie stood up and started yelling at the screen as if Ben could hear her. "Now you're sorry? Now that it doesn't matter anymore, you say you're sorry and you love us? Why in the world would you think we care if you're sorry?" Casey tried to calm her down but to no avail. She turned to Casey and continued ranting, "Why in the world would he say all that stuff to us at the end? Does he expect us to feel sorry for him? Or maybe he wanted everyone else to feel sorry for him." She started talking to everyone else in the room. "He ruined our lives! All of you think we were poor because of the way we lived, but we weren't poor. He had so much money, but he wouldn't spend a dime on us! We could have had a nice house and clothes. We could have gone on nice vacations and been a big part of the social life in our dinky little town! But no, *not Ben Crawford!* He just kept his greedy money to himself! Well, now that he's dead and gone, I want my money, and I want it now."

Mark and Casey took Cassie in the other room to calm her down so that they could continue with the reading of the will. Meanwhile, everyone else was talking to one another in the office and waiting for the three or them to come back. André got up and walked out to the waiting room. Deidre and Carissa followed her. André completely broke down. Through her sobs she tried to talk. "She didn't get what Ben was saying at all. He so wanted them to try to understand. I don't care what she says. People can change. Ben loved us."

As Deidre and Carissa were calming André down, Deidre remembered Ben's last days. About a week after Ben's test, he came down with pneumonia. He let Deidre take him to the doctor's office, but he refused to go to the hospital. "Can't you see that this is just God's way of speeding up the process of dying? No, I'm staying right here to die just like Annie did. She didn't want to die in some cold and white hospital, and neither do I." Ben wasn't left alone for a minute from that time to the day he died.

One day when Deidre arrived, she was surprised to see Ben dressed and sitting on the porch. As she was walking up to the house, Ben started getting up from his rocker. Sara came out from the house. "He's been waiting for you. He asked me to help get him dressed before you got here. But he wouldn't tell me why. He just said he would need a blanket."

When Deidre stepped onto the porch, she asked him, "What's up, Ben? What can I do for you?"

"I'd like you to take me to the park one last time, and I'd like to sit on Annie's and my bench."

Sara started to oppose the idea, but Deidre smiled. She held up her hand and then spoke to Ben. "I think that's a lovely idea, and it's such a beautiful spring day. I'm glad to see that you have a blanket because it's just a little chilly out." Sara was confused, but Deidre assured her that everything was fine. Deidre remembered the story that Ben had told her about him and Annie going to the park one last time before she died. So she knew exactly what Ben was doing. He was dying.

Before they left, Sara took Deidre to the side and whispered, "I wrote a letter to Ben's children a week ago to let them know the condition of their father. I gave it to Ben's lawyer because I heard he knew how to contact them in case of Ben's death. You know he's written them a couple times the past few months, but they haven't tried to contact him. They probably never even opened his letters." Deidre was surprised to hear that he had tried to contact them. She always assumed he didn't even know where or how to contact them.

Two days later Daniel called Deidre to let her know Ben had passed away in the middle of the night in his sleep. Brad helped Deidre make all the funeral arrangements, and Sara contacted the papers and Ben's lawyer. André cried when she got the suit out for the mortician to put on him. She remembered the day they had gone shopping and he had said he could wear the suit to his funeral. They had to wait several days before they could have the funeral because Ben's children lived so far away.

One evening Deidre's family gathered for dinner at her house. They got out pictures with Ben that they had taken the last year on different occasions. André got an idea for the funeral. "Grandma, let's make up some memory boards with pictures on them for Ben's funeral. The only problem is the only pictures we have are the ones of him with our family."

Deidre thought it was a nice idea. "Ben showed me a picture album. I can go get it tomorrow, and we can add them to the memory boards." Deidre had a photo shooting the next day in Richmond, so she was going that way anyway. She decided to go to Ben's on the way back home. When she got to Ben's house, she found Sara, John, and Daniel cleaning the yard and the house. They had also cleaned up around the grave site. "Why didn't you let me know that you were going to do this? My family would have come to help. I'm sorry I didn't even think about doing any of this." Sara told her it wasn't that big of a deal. Deidre couldn't believe how nice the porch looked. Sara had taken a lot of stuff off the porch. "I put a lot of the stuff in the shed and barn. And then there are some things I packed up." She had also cleaned the inside of the house and opened the windows. "I packed a lot of things up that were in here too. I only threw away things that were worn out like blankets and pillows and some really nasty curtains that were stored in one of the spare bedrooms." Neither Deidre nor Sara thought anyone would mind since Ben's children really didn't want anything to do with anything.

Deidre didn't hear John walk up behind her, so it startled her when he said, "Hi, Deidre. How are you and the girls doing?"

After her heart settled down, she smiled. "As well as to be expected. Thanks for asking. How are all of you doing?" John told her they were about the same way. She turned to Sara to ask for her help. "Sara, Ben showed me a photo album once. Do you know where it is? André, Carissa, and I are making memory boards, and we thought it would be nice to put the pictures that are in the album on one of the boards."

Sara thought it was a great idea and went and got the album for her. She also fetched some other picture that were in a box. "I have some picture at home. And we have four or five easels in the store that we use to hold signs. I'll go get them if you have time." Deidre suggested that she could go with her, but John asked Deidre if she could stay because he wanted to show her a few things. So she agreed to wait there for Sara to return.

After Sara left, John took Deidre to the grave site. She couldn't believe her eyes. John and Daniel had cut trees away and cleared a large area away. John had also made a nice headstone for Ben. "I wanted to make a bigger one, but Sara said that his headstone should be the same size as Annie's." He explained to Deidre that he had made Annie's stone as well.

"Oh, John, this is all so perfect. I agree with Sara that it looks nice having both stones the same size. I didn't know you made Annie's stone."

John explained to her that he had made a lot of the headstones for the community. "I don't make anything fancy, just simple ones. They're usually for private grave sites or family graveyards. I also make headstones for people's pets. Ben told me what he wanted on his stone years ago. 'Gone to Be with Annie. Ben.'"

Then there was the date of birth and death. Deidre also noticed a cherub on the top of each stone, and they were facing each other. The cherub wasn't on Annie's stone before. "I like the cherubs on each of the stones. Did you make those too?"

John answered, "No, we sell those in our store. It's just a little added touch. Daniel and I are going to dig the grave in the morning." Deidre was glad the hole wasn't there yet.

John then took Deidre to show her the other things they had gotten done. Deidre was completely amazed by all the work they had done. They had cut the grass and trimmed around the shed and the barn. They cleared some more land away that had been overgrown. She had never noticed before that there were some smaller shacks back in the woods. John pointed to each shack and explained to her what they were. "There are a couple of old chicken coops, a wood shed, and an outhouse." She asked John if there was anything else back there. "Matter of fact, there is. Would you like to go look?"

Deidre really wasn't dressed for it, but she was really curious and wanted to see what was back there. "Sure! Do you think it's all right that I walk back there like this? I don't have my tennis shoes or boots on?"

He told her she should be fine. "Things look far away, but they're not really. They're just behind the house, so we'll take another route back to the house afterward." John was right. It wasn't really that far. She got a good look at the coops, woodshed, and then there was another medium shed. John told her, "That's where they kept the pigs, and then there was a beautiful creek just on the other side of the shacks and then all the land on the other side of the creek. I love this property. It once was a really nice piece of property. Ben worked this farm awfully hard when he was younger."

Deidre could envision Ben working his farm and land. No wonder he didn't have time for his family. There was a lot of work to do. She remembered Ben telling her once that he had no one to help him on the farm … and that Casey refused to do any work on the farm. So he had him just cut grass.

On the way back to the house, Deidre saw for the first time what the back of the house looked like. The house was in pretty good shape for its age and lack of upkeep. She could imagine Ben, Annie and the twins living in it. It was so sad that the twins couldn't see what they really had. The land, farm, house, animals—yes, it was a simple life, but it was a good life.

As they rounded the corner of the house, Deidre could see Sara waiting for her. As Sara and Deidre sat on the porch and went through the pictures, Sara explained to her what each of the pictures were about and who the people were. Sara also went over the pictures that were in the box. Sara didn't know everyone, but she knew a lot. "The people I don't know personally I know because Annie and Ben told me who they were. I can't tell you how many times Ben has showed me these pictures in the box." Deidre wondered why Ben showed her the pictures in the photo album but none of the ones in the box. Sara suggested that since they were having the funeral right there at the grave site, they could put two easels on each side or his casket. Then they would place flowers on each side of the headstone. Deidre agreed that her ideas sounded nice.

Sara, Deidre, and the girls had put a nice luncheon together for after the funeral. There wasn't very many people coming, but they wanted everything to look nice for Ben's children. They waited an hour after the funeral was to start for Ben's children to arrive. When they arrived, they had their spouses with them, and they immediately took their seats in the front and never said a word or showed any emotions of any kind. They never walked up to the casket or looked at any of the pictures. After the short funeral service, they walked up to the lawyer and made plans for the reading of the will. And then they told him they didn't want to see the house or be a part of the wake.

Deidre's family didn't come to the funeral because she thought Ben's children might feel uncomfortable with a bunch of strangers there. When they left, Deidre called Brad and told him to get everyone together and come celebrate Ben's memory with them. It ended up being a very nice wake, and everyone loved the memory boards and the headstone that John had made.

As Deidre was leaving, she stopped and turned around to see the house one last time. She doubted that she would ever see it again. She missed seeing Ben sitting on the porch in his rocker. She started back to the car and whispered to herself, "Bye, Ben. I'll miss you deeply."

CHAPTER 15

Everyone was gathered back into the office for the reading of the will. André wasn't sure she wanted to be there, but Mark told her that it was mandatory for her to be there. "We've come this far, André, so let's wrap up everything Ben wanted us to do, okay?"

Deidre along with everyone else in the office had no idea what to expect. Whatever was going to happen, Deidre felt that Cassie wasn't going to like any of it.

After he read the formalities of the will, Mark jumped right into what Ben was going to give to Cassie and Casey. "Ben sold a lot of his land off so that the two of you wouldn't have to wait for your inheritance."

Cassie had to make her hateful comment. "Well, it's about time he did something right."

You could tell everyone was just as disgusted with her as André was. André made a comment under her breath but loud enough so that Cassie could hear it. "Too bad she can't finally do something right and shut up."

Cassie jerked her head around to give André a nasty look but didn't say anything to her.

Mark continued with the reading. "Ben left each of you 2,500,000 dollars each, which you will receive in a certified check today before you leave the office. The bank has agreed to cash it for you before you leave to go home."

Casey made a gasping noise, but you could tell Cassie wasn't happy at all. "Are we supposed to be happy with that? I know for a fact that between the money he had and the land, there is a lot more money than that. Who's going to get the rest of our money? These moochers sitting here? Well, let me tell you right now that that's just not going to happen."

Casey stood up and spoke to her louder than anyone had heard him speak since he had been there. "Cassie, we left Dad and Mom a long time ago. We never tried to communicate with them, not even Mom, except for a few hateful letters you wrote to her. We should be happy with what we're getting. I think it's more than fair."

"*Fair?* What in the world are you talking about? You may be happy, but I want my rightful share for the miserable life he made us live!"

Casey put his hand on Cassie's arm and spoke in a softer tone. "Cassie, I think we made him and Mom more miserable when we left and never communicated with them than you think. I think you got back at him and Mom years ago. You've got to let it go and move on. Let's take our share of the money and get as far away from here as we can and never look back … ever again."

Cassie couldn't let that happen. "I want to hear how much of my money all these losers are going to get. I just don't think I can let this happen. They're not even related to him like we are."

Casey disagreed with her. "Maybe not by blood, but I think since Dad no longer had us or Mom, he found another family for himself. It sounds like there was a lot of love between them. Between Deidre and her family and the Matthews, Dad was well taken care of, and so was the house and property. We stopped being his family, so he found another family that loved him. I think he really changed, but we weren't here to see it. We didn't want to see it."

Cassie just stared at her brother. "We could have been that family if he would have let us. When we were little, we were that family. And then when we grew up, he shut us out and gave us nothing."

"No, Cassie, when we grew up, we didn't like farm life. We wanted more. And that's when we shut Dad out, and Mom had to suffer from it. Now please let's just go home. I'm done with all this. I'm leaving with my share of the money."

Cassie didn't seem as irate as before, but she still wasn't completely sold on it all. "We're going to at least stay and hear what everyone else gets, aren't we?"

Mark spoke up. "I'm sorry, but in the will Ben states that after each person hears what they receive as their inheritance, then they are to leave the room."

Cassie was upset all over again. "Is it that bad that he knows how mad we'll be if we hear how much he gave them?"

Mark continued to explain, "No, that's not the reason he wants each of you to leave. I probably shouldn't say this, but you and your brother received the largest amount. No one else will receive anything near what you two have received."

Casey once again took Cassie's arm. "Please, Cassie, let's just take our money and go home. There's nothing left for us here."

Cassie finally gave in and agreed to go. "You're right. There's nothing here for us. They've taken everything else that belongs to us." She looked around at everyone and left the room with her brother.

After they left, Mark explained that Ben wanted the rest of them to hear what he had left his children so that all of them could be witnesses to what the twins received, but now that it was the Matthews' turn, Deidre and girls would have to leave the room while he told the Matthews what they were receiving.

When the Matthew family came out of the office, John was shaking his head. Deidre and Carissa stood up, but André remained sitting. "I don't understand why Ben left us so much. He left us the rest of the land that the house sits on up to the creek and a million dollars for Sara and me and five hundred thousand dollars for Daniel. In my wildest dreams, I had no idea that Ben had that much money." John wanted to go on, but then Mark asked Deidre and the girls to come in next.

Deidre had mixed feelings as she sat to listen to what Mark was about to say. "Ben wanted to make the three of you last because this was going to take a little longer than the others. But I doubt that it will take as long as it did with Casey and Cassie since there was an argument."

Deidre and Carissa chuckled, but when Deidre looked over at André, she had a very sober face.

Mark opened a file and handed each of them a letter. "These are letters that Ben wrote to each of you but then asked if June, my assistant, would type them up for him. June thought you would want the handwritten ones as well. So she slipped those in each of the envelopes along with the typed ones. You can read them later when you're alone and have the time."

Deidre watched as Mark handed each of the girls their letters. She finally saw a smile on André's face, but it left the moment Mark started speaking again. "I know it's been an extremely long day, so let me get to the will and let you know what Ben left each of you."

André stopped him to ask a question. "Before you start can you tell us why he left us anything at all? We only knew him for about a year, and we didn't do anything to deserve anything. I have to agree with Cassie that whatever he left us belongs to her and her brother."

Deidre placed her hand on André's wrist and was about to say something, but Mark spoke first. "I believe the letters will tell you why, but let me say something on Ben's behalf. The three of you showered Ben with more love than he could have ever imagined. Casey hit the nail on the head when he said that Ben found a new family that loved him, and he loved all of you. You brought so much joy to his life at the end, and this is his way of saying thank you. Consider this a gift he left for each of you. You wouldn't want to disrespect his memory by not wanting the gift he left you, would you?"

André lowered her head and answered Mark, "No, I wouldn't want that." She looked up at Mark and Deidre, and then she said, "I did love him. I loved him very much." Deidre agreed that they all did. André continued, "I never thought of this as a gift from him. I just thought he felt he owed it to us to leave us something, and I didn't want that. Thank you for clearing that up for me." André smiled and asked, "So what's the gift he left me?" Everyone laughed.

Mark explained that Carissa was first to receive her inheritance. "To Carissa, my little artist, I leave five hundred thousand dollars. I hope this will pay off your student loan and make it so that you can continue your education debt-free. Plus you should have some extra for yourself to help pay for your wedding dress and wedding. I wish I could have been there for the wedding, but it was time for me to be with my Annie."

All Carissa could do was shake her head in disbelief. "I don't believe this. That's so much money." She looked over at her grandmother and André. "Do you believe this? And this all happened because we were trespassing?" The three of them laughed.

Mark looked over at André and then started reading the will again. "To André, Missy, I leave five hundred thousand dollars. Maybe this will make it so you can start the daycare center that you've talked about."

Boy did that shock Deidre. She had never heard anything about André wanting to open a daycare center. It shocked Carissa as well. "I never knew you wanted to open a daycare. Why have you never talked to me about this?"

André looked over at her cousin. "It's nothing exciting like being an artist or doing something great with your art. It's just a daycare."

"Just a daycare? I think it's great that you have a plan for your future. You always acted like you didn't know what you wanted to do with your future. I know you love kids, and you're so good with then. But I never thought of a daycare. That's a fantastic idea!"

Deidre was always so proud of how the two girls were always so supportive of each other. She was happy for both of them.

Mark had to get their attention. "I'm sorry, but we need to move on. It's getting late." Once he got their attention, he continued to read the will. "To Deidre, you're like a daughter to me. I leave twenty acres of land that is located on the other side of the creek. I was told how much it is worth, but I didn't sell it with the other property because I thought you could choose to lease it out or save it and sell it later for more money than what it's worth now. Or you can sell it now. It was the property that you thought was so beautiful. I also leave you five hundred thousand dollars. Maybe you can expand Special Moments and even hire André to be a photographer for you. I'm just saying." The three of them laughed again. Deidre could hear Ben's humor coming across, but she also heard his seriousness at the same time.

Mark once again asked for their attention. "There's one more thing that Ben left all three of you."

The three of them looked at one another, confused. Deidre spoke up. "He left something else for the three of us."

Carissa chimed in, "Like to share or what?"

Mark chuckled. "Well, that's what I'm about to tell you." Mark continued to read. "I leave to Deidre, Carissa, and André all the contents in my house." Now the three of them were really confused, but before they could say anything, Mark continued to read, "I know what you're thinking. *Why would you want all my junky old stuff?* But I assure you there's more than you think. Don't forget to go into the attic. There's only one condition I'm making. I want the three of you to go together when you go through the house and up in the attic. Anything you don't want, you can ask Sara if she wants it because she has garage sales a few times a year. And if she doesn't want it, just get rid of it. The house belongs to John, so I don't know if it will be torn down or what."

Mark stopped reading. "That's all there is. Once you read your letters, you might understand more. You each will receive your checks here before you leave, and the bank has been notified that you will be cashing them there. I assure you that it will be a lot quicker if you cash your checks at Ben's bank. I have some papers for you to sign, and each of you will take a copy with you. I advise each of you to get with an accountant or lawyer and have them help you with your investments and learn about inheritance taxes. If you don't have anyone to help you, I can represent you or direct you to someone."

Deidre told him that they had a family lawyer, but she still thanked him for everything. Each of them shook his hand before they left. As Mark was shaking André's hand, he asked if she was okay. "Well, we made it through the tape like you promised Ben. I'm sorry it didn't turn out the way you had hoped. You can pick up the tape at June's desk."

André didn't know what to say, and she was afraid if she did say something, she might start crying, so she simply said, "Thank you for everything."

Each of them picked up their checks, and André picked up the tape. June told them about writing the letters. "Ben didn't think you would be able to read his writing, and he had scratched out things and misspelled words, so that's why he asked me to type the letters out. But I thought each of you would like the original letters. It was hard to type out the letters because they were so emotional. He loved you guys so much. As far as he was concerned, you were his family."

They thanked her and walked out of the office. Evening had come. André couldn't believe it took a whole day to watch the tape and read the will. It should have taken only a few hours at the most. As they were walking around the corner of the building to get to their car, they saw Cassie leaning against a car. They could see Casey sitting in the backseat of the car.

Carissa was totally disgusted with her. "You have got to be kidding. What does she want now? I'm so done with her and all the antics that she pulled today. I'm going over there right now to tell her to get lost."

Deidre stopped her. "Why don't you go to the car while I go see what's up?" Carissa was reluctant, but she obeyed her grandmother.

André wasn't as upset as Carissa. "Grandma, do you mind if I go with you? I promise not to cause any problems. I actually feel sorry for her."

Deidre said it was all right and told Carissa they'd be right back. "I'm not staying here by myself I'm going too. Don't worry. I promise to keep my mouth shut." As they started to walk, Carissa had to add, "I hope." Deidre stopped to look at her as Carissa said, "I'm just saying." That made each of them chuckle.

When they approached the car, Deidre addressed them. "Cassie—" Then she bent down and looked at Casey in the car. "Casey," she said. Casey nodded to her but remained in the car. Since Cassie didn't say anything, Deidre decided to start the conversation. "I assume you're here to find out what each of us received in the inheritance. We really don't want to make matters worse, but we really can't share that with you."

Cassie threw her cigarette down on the ground and stepped on it. "I have to admit I'd really like to know what you got, but that's not why I stayed."

Deidre couldn't believe how calm Cassie sounded. She seemed like a whole different person than the one they had put up with all day. "Then why are you still here?"

Cassie looked from Deidre to André. "I'd like to talk to her for a moment ... alone."

Deidre didn't like the idea, but André stepped toward Cassie and turned to her grandmother. "It'll be find, Grandma. Why don't you and Carissa go back to the car, and I'll be there shortly." As they left, André turned to Cassie. "I'm glad we're able to have a chance to talk."

Cassie was taken aback by André's reaction. She thought she would be irritated with her, but she sounded more sympathetic toward her than irritated. "You want to talk to me?"

André nodded and said, "Yes, I've wanted to talk to you all day. But we got off on the wrong foot, and it made it impossible for us to talk to each other. I'm so sorry for all the hateful comments I made toward you today. It was wrong of me to do that, especially at a time like now when emotions are so high in the first place."

Cassie stopped André before she could go on. "It works both ways. But I didn't stay to talk about being sorry. I need to know about my dad. What was he like at the end? I need to know if he ever talked about me and my brother. I know what he said to us at the end of the tape, but I guess I need to know more."

André wasn't sure exactly what Cassie wanted to know, but she decided to just start telling her what Ben shared with her about his feelings. "Frist and foremost, Cassie, you need to know your father loved the both of you very much." André's attention turned to Casey as he got out of the car and started walking around to the front of the car to join them. "He said it more than once. But I'll be honest with you. He was also upset with you. He felt so helpless when it came to trying to reach the two of you. He talked about when you were young, and he showed us pictures. He was always looking at his picture album. You heard the story about our relationship with him, but there was so much more he didn't put in the tape. We adored him, and he clung to every little bit of love and attention he could get. He made us laugh and was always there to listen to everything we needed to talk about. He had a way of getting you to talk. He didn't always give advice, but he had a way of suggesting something that would make you start thinking about what you were going through. I know what you said about him, and when he talked about the past, I could hear your side of him in his stories. But I also heard his side. I wish you could have heard his side of the story."

Cassie then showed André a letter. "I did. He wrote both of us a letter to read later, but I decided to read it before I left. I never wanted to hear his side of story. I was so consumed in what I didn't have and what I thought life should be for us. I hated farm life. We hated farm life. I'll never agree to the way he wouldn't spend his money to make our life a little better. I never thought about the fact that he loved the simple life and didn't understand why we didn't. He didn't want all the hustle and bustle of the busy outside life. He loved his life, and he didn't want to watch us get caught up in a material world. The only problem was he never asked us. He didn't even want us to have friends because they could have influenced us in the wrong way. He should have talked to us and not just dictated to us." Cassie's voice was rising higher and higher as she talked. Casey gently touched her arm. "I know now he changed, but at that point we didn't want anything to do with him. I wish we could have gotten to know that person on the tape and the person you knew, but we were too selfish and carried a lot of hate inside us for him. Even this letter he wrote to us is not the person we once knew. I know we can't go back, but I'm really glad we had the chance to see the tape. We no longer need to carry around all that hate and anger."

André was smiling from ear to ear. "That's exactly what Ben wanted to do when we made the tape. He wanted to let you know how sorry he was and that he wished he could have changed things. He wanted to let you know he had changed, and most of all he wanted you to know he loved you very much."

Casey spoke up this time. "We know that the house doesn't belong to us and that nothing inside it belongs to us, but we'd like to see and go in the house one last time. We know we could have seen it the day of the funeral, and we're sorry we were so rude to everyone. But now after today we'd really like to look around one last time."

André knew she probably should ask her grandmother first, but it didn't feel right to say that at the moment. Besides, knowing her grandmother, she knew she wouldn't mind. "I think that would be great. If you can give me a number to reach you at, we can meet you there. The house is locked up now that there's no one there." André hoped they wouldn't be upset that she couldn't let them go by themselves to the house. Casey gave her his cell number. "We don't mean to rush anyone, but we need to leave in a couple of days. Our spouses have already gone home, and I need to get back to work soon."

André handed Cassie her letter back and returned to her car. She was so excited when she explained everything to her grandmother and Carissa. "They've had a change of heart. Ben's plan worked." As Deidre was driving home, André shared with them everything that was said. Then she got to the part about their request. "They have to leave in a couple of days, but before they do, they would like to meet us at the house and see it and the property one last time."

Deidre was concerned about their request, and Carissa let them know about her feelings. "Now it all makes sense. They're just acting like they care. What they really want is to see what's in the house. I wished you hadn't told them that no one was there. Now they can break the door down and take what they want. You heard what Ben said. Some of the things are valuable."

Deidre didn't agree with Carissa. "I don't think they'd do anything like that, but I don't understand why they'd want to see the house. Even if they feel differently about Ben, that doesn't change the fact that they hated living there."

André didn't care about the reason for any of it. She was just happy that Ben's wish came true. "Even if they do want more, I don't think there's anything wrong with that. It all belongs to them in the first place. But I'm hoping for the best. I hope that they've changed their feelings about everything. That's what Ben wanted, and so do I."

It was quiet the rest of the ride home as the three of them thought about the day and what had transpired. André decided to read her letter from Ben on the way home. The letter thanked her for her love and told her how much she meant to him. As she continued to read, she had tears in her eyes and a smile on her face.

CHAPTER 16

Deidre called Sara early the next morning before they opened the store. Since the land and house legally belonged to her and John, she thought they should make arrangement with her. "I don't know if you know that Ben left everything in the house to the girls and me."

Sara told her, "Yes, we know. In the letter Ben wrote to us, he explained that he would like for us to grant you access to the house for as long as you need so that the three of you could go through the house. You know we don't have a problem with that."

Deidre thanked her and continued, "Did he explain that we'll give you most of the things inside to sell. Plus we'll pay to have anything hauled away that you don't what."

Sara confirmed what Deidre said. "Yes, he explained all that to us, but there's no need for you to pay to haul anything away. We'll handle all that. We're not in a hurry. I think John is focusing on the property first. I doubt that we will do anything with the house until later. We may even wait until next year. There's just so much we need to talk about and look into."

Deidre was so happy that John inherited the property. He had talked about how much he loved the property. She then informed Sara about what had happened after she and the girls had left the law office. She told her about André talking with the twins and how Cassie's attitude changed after she read her letter from Ben. "Sara, Casey and Cassie would like to look at the house and land one more time. I told André I'd call you to get permission. we'd meet with them there, of course, and I hope you'd be able to be there too."

Sara was quiet for a moment, and Deidre was somewhat afraid that she might have offended her in some way. "I don't understand. Why do they now want to see everything when at the funeral they didn't even take the time to look at their parents' headstones? It all sounds very strange to me."

Deidre agreed. "I said the exact same thing when André told me about their request, but André feels they have a right to one last visit to their home."

"But they hated that place. Why would they want to return to a place that gives them nothing but bad memories? Does any of this make sense to you, Deidre, because I'm really confused and leery of it all?"

Deidre understood how she felt, but she hoped she wouldn't let that stop them from letting the twins visit their home one last time. "I'm not sure what's going on. Maybe they're looking for some kind of forgotten memory that was good or maybe some closure. I was just hoping maybe we could let them look around tomorrow morning if you don't mind. And I was hoping maybe you could be there for any questions they may have."

Sara wasn't sure what to do. "You know we don't mind if you want to go to the house. You don't need our permission to show them around. But I don't know, Deidre, about me being there. They've let us know over and over again how much they dislike John and me. Besides, what kind of questions would they need to ask me? The mornings are really busy for me, so I'm just not sure if I can make it."

Deidre really would feel better if Sara was there with them. "I think you might be surprised at the way their attitudes have changed, and since they were asking André questions about their father, maybe you might be able to answer a lot more questions they have about their father too. I understand how busy you are, but I would really appreciate it if you could be there."

Sara reluctantly said she'd meet with them, so Deidre told André that she could call Casey and make the arrangements. Deidre thought that after the twins left, she and the girls could start going through the house. She had no idea how long it would take for them to go through everything.

Deidre and the girls arrived an hour earlier than scheduled so that they would be ready for the twins when they arrived. Sara was already there, working in the flower garden.

André was glad Sara was there. "Boy, you sure are an early bird, aren't you? I'm up but I sure can't see working this early but everything sure looks nice. Ben loved Annie's flower garden."

Sara got up from the ground and brushed the dirt off her pants. "I've been working this flower garden for years. I've added a lot of flowers to this garden in the past years. I don't have much of a garden at home, so this makes up for it. I never thought that one day this would be my garden."

André was happy for Sara, but it sounded so strange to hear Sara call the flower garden hers when she always heard Ben refer to it as Annie's garden.

Sara continued telling them what their plans were next for the property. "John and Daniel are going to first plow and plant a garden on the other side of the barn, and they're going to finish clearing trees and brush away from behind the house. This fall or next spring, John wants to start clearing some of the debris away in the woods. You should hear how excited he is about this land. He's always wanted a farm, and now he has one."

Deidre was wondering what their long-term plans were for the house and land. "Isn't that a lot for him to do along with the store? Are you guys planning on living here?"

Sara smiled. "John talked to Daniel and decided it was time to hand the store over to the next generation. Daniel and Carissa are ecstatic about having the store. Daniel's education in business management will help him a lot. They plan on having full-time help and maybe even expanding the store to include a larger hardware section since that's in such demand." Sara stopped for a minute and looked around. "As for living here, the answer is yes. We plan on living here, but we're not sure if we will update this house or just tear it down and rebuild. Like I said before, there's a lot we need to look into."

Deidre was so happy to hear that the property was once again going to come alive. Ben knew exactly what he was doing when he left it all to John and Sara.

The twins arrived right on time, which was a lot better than last time when they were an hour late for their father's funeral. Casey was walking ahead of Cassie, and they were talking about the flower garden as they walked up to the house. When they reached Deidre and Sara, Casey reached his hand out to Sara to shake her hand. "Hi, Sara, we were so glad to hear you were going to be here today in case we had any questions. I know you're busy with the store, so we really appreciate you taking the time for us."

Sara was in shock as she shook his hand. "No problem. I wanted to come and work in the flower garden anyway." She noticed it was Casey doing all the talking instead of Cassie for a change.

"Cassie and I were talking about how beautiful the garden looked as we were walking up. So you're the master gardener that did all this. Mom loved this garden, but I imagine you've added a lot more flowers over time. It's beautiful."

Sara thanked him and then looked at Cassie. "Hi, Cassie, I'm glad both of you came today."

Cassie wasn't as friendly as Casey, but she wasn't being her normal rude self either. "Since you're still working in the garden, I take it that you and John inherited the land and house."

Sara was hoping this wasn't going to start a debate on who should have what and why. "Yes, we did. From the street to the creek. I promise you that your parents' grave site will always be taken care of."

Cassie nodded to her and then turned to Deidre. "Good morning, Deidre. Thank you for allowing us to come." She then turned to Sara. "I guess you're the one we should thank since this is now all yours."

Sara couldn't read Cassie's attitude. Was she being nice, or was she leading to something? She was starting to think that the real reason that the twins were there was to find out who got what from Ben.

André and Carissa stepped down from the porch where they had been sitting. Cassie noticed them immediately. "Wow, looks like everyone came. Is it because of us being here, or is there something else going on?"

Carissa didn't like all the questions that Cassie was asking. "André came since she made all the arrangements, and I came along for the ride since I'm meeting up with Daniel for lunch."

Cassie looked at her strangely as if she wasn't sure she believed her. "Yeah, I noticed you and Sara's kid were really cozy during the hearing. I take it the two of you are an item."

Carissa was very proud to announce that they were engaged. Cassie's eyes lifted as she commented, "Interesting! So all of this may belong to the two of you someday?"

Carissa was about to answer her when Casey interrupted, "That's really none of our business, Cassie. Don't forget we're here to look around one last time, not to pry into everyone's personal life. We need to get started because we fly out this evening." Casey turned to André and thanked her for making all the arrangements and then asked Deidre and Sara if they wouldn't mind walking around with them. "Could we walk around the property first?"

They started around toward the shed and barn. Casey was asking all the questions as he and Deidre walked ahead of Cassie and Sara. "Is there anything planted on the other side of the barn right now?"

Sara explained what was happening. "It's all overgrown right now. But John and Daniel will be here later today to start plowing and planting. It's a little late in the year, but he thought he might plant at least part of the land. Next year we'll plant the whole thing."

Cassie started with the questions again. "That's a lot to do when you have a store to run. You do plan on keeping your store, don't you? I take it that's your main source of income."

Sara was done giving out personal information to Cassie. "We don't have any idea what we're going to do at this point."

Cassie wasn't going to give up. "Yea, but—"

Casey stopped her from going any further. "Cassie, enough with the questions. It's none of your business, so just drop it." He turned to Sara. "I apologize for Cassie. She's always like this. She always asks a hundred questions even about the littlest things."

Casey asked to look in the shed. Cassie then said, "Why would you want to go in there? There was nothing about that place that we ever liked."

Casey refreshed her memory. "You don't remember when we would play hide-and-seek in there? Or how about the little hiding place we made in there for when we would hide from Mom and Dad?"

For once there was a smile on Cassie's face. "Oh, my goodness, I totally forgot all about that!"

They were sad when they walked in the shed. It was so old now, and you could tell not much went on in there any longer. They looked over to where their hiding place was. "I remember how much we loved to come in here when it rained or stormed. I would come in here with my dolls and hide. I remember one time when I was in here, Dad came in to get something. I thought it was so neat that he didn't even see me. Then just when he was walking out the door, he said, 'Your mother is looking for you, Cassie,' and he left. We never fooled them for a minute."

After they left the shed, Casey stopped and looked at the barn, but they decided there was nothing there that they wanted to see. Then they started walking toward the creek behind the house. Deidre watched as Casey took Cassie's hand and led her. She could picture them as children and Casey doing the exact same thing back then. They stopped right before they got to a large tree. They both looked up. Deidre and Sara looked up to see what they were looking at and saw the remainder of a rather large tree house. The twins couldn't believe that any of it was still there.

Casey started explaining to Deidre and Sara about the tree house. "We begged our father to make us a tree house, but our Mother was so afraid we'd fall and break a bone."

Cassie chimed in, "Which you did. You broke your leg, and I got the tree house all to myself for a while. You got so mad the first time you could go up to the tree house and found that I put dollies, a rug, and curtains in it, and I had most of my dolls up there. Mom helped me decorate it and told me that once you were better, I'd have to change it back."

Casey added, "I let you keep the curtains and rug, but the dollies and dolls had to go except for Betsey." He explained to Deidre and Sara that Betsey was Cassie's favorite doll and that it went everywhere she went.

Cassie smiled at the memory of her doll. "When I had to go to school, my mother would let me put her on her rocking chair on the porch. She assured me that Betsey would be there waiting for me when I got home, and she always was. It's funny, but I don't remember what happened to that doll."

Casey interrupted Cassie's memories by taking her arm. "Look, Cassie. The swing tree next to the creek is still there." The swing was gone, but the tree was still there. He told Deidre and Sara the story of the swing. "Dad put up a tire swing in the tree, and Mom was afraid we would jump from the tree to the creek and hurt ourselves."

Once again Cassie jumped in. "Which you did. You had to have ten stitches in your head. We also used the tire swing to climb up the tree. I could always climb higher than you could."

Casey talked about how they swam in the creek when it was really hot out. "Mom never wanted us to swim in the creek unless she was back here to watch us."

Cassie added, "I remember when Dad would sneak up on us when we were playing out here and throw us in the creek. We loved it, but Mom would get so mad because we had our play clothes on. But it never stopped Dad from doing it again."

Deidre wondered how the two of them could hate a place so much yet have so many great memories. She hoped they were both listening to themselves, realizing how nice they had it—simple but nice.

Casey asked if they could go to the grave site before they looked inside the house. Deidre agreed and pointed the way.

It was easier if everyone walked single file, so Casey led the way. Cassie walked right behind him. As they were walking through the woods, Cassie reminded Casey of the trails. "Remember when we would go for walks in the woods? It would really be hard to do that now that everything is so overgrown."

Casey stopped and turned to Cassie. "Remember when we ran away because Dad wouldn't let us have another dog?" He explained to Deidre and Sara, "We had one dog, but it stayed outside, so we wanted a house dog. Dad wasn't going to let that happen because he knew i Mom would have to take care of it and not us. He was right, but you couldn't tell us that at the time."

Cassie laughed as she continued the story. "We didn't want to walk by the road because Casey said Dad would find us, so we started walking through the woods. We had only walked the woods once before with Mom, and she had packed a picnic for us. Anyway, we had packed fruit and some crackers, and off we went. We thought we had gone a long way, and I was starting to get scared because it was getting dark. Casey assured me we were okay, and then we heard a noise and thought it was a wild animal that was going to eat us. That did it for me. I started crying."

Casey joined in and said, "And that made me start crying and the next thing we knew Dad was there to rescue us. Years later we found out that it was Dad that made the noises so that we would be ready to come home when he showed up. That was pretty smart when you think about it."

When they arrived at the clearing where their parents were buried, Casey once again took Cassie's hand. They stopped, and they were quiet for a moment. Once Casey spoke, Deidre wasn't sure if he was speaking to Cassie or everyone. "Everything looks very nice." Then he and Cassie walked up to the headstones. Casey asked about the headstone. "I heard John made Mom's headstone. Did he make Dad's too?"

Sara told them yes.

Cassie swayed her hand over the cherubs. "I like the cherubs and the way they're looking at each other." Then she looked up at Deidre. "Now let me get this straight. You found Mom's grave site before you met Dad, and you cleared some of the trees and stuff away. Is that right?" Deidre nodded yes. Cassie continued, "Why? I mean what drove you here in the first place, and why clear a total stranger's grave site?"

Deidre chuckled as she commented on Cassie's questions. "It's really hard to explain, and I'm not sure you would understand even if I could explain it. I look at it as what we call *a God thing*. That's when God is the one who is in control of it all."

Cassie glanced at her mother's headstone and commented, "I know what *a God thing* is. I heard my mother use that phrase a number of times when we were growing up. I haven't heard it since we left this place.

Casey looked down at his watch. "Wow, we really need to speed it up if we want to see the inside of the house before we leave."

They quickly left the woods and were once again at the house. They were pleasantly surprised when they got there. André and Carissa had made some sandwiches for everyone. André spoke up when she saw them. "There was some food left over from the funeral, so we thought maybe everyone would like something to eat."

Deidre asked Sara why she hadn't taken any of the food home with her after the funeral.

"I knew people would be coming and going for a while, so I thought it would be nice if there was food here for whoever was here." That sounded so much like Sara. She was always looking out for others.

Casey was concerned about eating when they were so pressed for time. "Thanks, but if we want to see the house, we really need to look quickly."

André suggested that they put a sandwich on a plate and take it with them as they looked. They both thought that was a good idea and thanked the girls for the sandwiches. As Casey was fixing a sandwich, Cassie was looking around at the kitchen. "Everything is so old. It's a mess compared to what I remember."

Sara told her about how Ben became like a recluse and wouldn't let her do very much to the house. "He'd let me do a little cleaning in the kitchen and bath once in a while. He'd call and order groceries and have them delivered. We always added a lot more than what he ordered. There would be times when he'd let me dust and change the bedsheets. I would stay and sit on the porch with him when he would let me. He became thinner and thinner, and then there was the stroke. And soon after that, arthritis set in, and he wouldn't exercise, so he could barely walk from the house to the porch."

Casey handed Cassie a sandwich, and they walked into the living room to look around. They noticed that the curtains looked fairly new, and so did some of the pillows and covers that covered the furniture. Cassie spotted the picture of Ben. "Carissa, is this the picture that you received a ribbon for?" Carissa told her it was. Then Cassie saw the picture of her mother's grave site. "Oh, my mom's gravesite was a mess once, wasn't it?" Casey joined Cassie and started looking at the pictures with her.

Carissa explained the picture in more detail. "After this picture was taken is when we cleared some of the debris away, and then later that day after we met Ben, we took him there." Cassie shook her head in disbelief. She still didn't understand why they did what they did.

On the couch were the memory boards that Deidre and the girls had put together for the funeral. Casey and Cassie started going through the pictures and remembered when a lot of them had been taken. After a few minutes, Deidre stepped up to the two of them. "All these pictures are yours to take with you. Some were in a photo album, and others were in a box. You can take them all with you and divide them up between the two of you. The only pictures we want are the ones on this board that show him when he was with us."

Casey looked at Cassie. "I'd like to have some of these. How about you?" Cassie continued to look at the pictures as she agreed with Casey. Deidre asked André to take the pictures off the boards and put them in a box for the twins. Meanwhile, they were going upstairs to look around.

As they were going up the steps, Cassie commented on how bad everything looked. "How could he have lived like this? The stairs are so creaky, and the walls have cracks in them everywhere, not to mention the walls are so dingy-looking going up these stairs."

Casey gave her his thoughts about it all. "It's been a long time since we've been here. Things get old. Besides, he could no longer take care of things. Not to mention I don't think he cared anymore. At least the living room walls are painted."

Once they were upstairs, each of them wanted to go see their bedrooms, so Deidra went with Casey, and Sara went with Cassie.

As Casey entered his room, he was disappointed with what he saw. "It looks so different, but at the same time, it looks the same. Does that make any sense? I don't think anyone's been in here for years." Deidre didn't answer because she felt he was just expressing his feelings.

There were other things in his room besides his things that his parents had stored in there. He walked up to his bed and sat on it. "I always loved it when I would get up in the morning and sit on the side of the bed and look out the window." As he looked around, he suddenly got very excited. "Oh no, I don't believe what I'm seeing." He got up and walked up to some shelves. He took a couple of things off of it and turned to Deidre. "They kept my toys!" Then he turned back around to the shelf. "Here's my baseball mitt, my ball, and even my baseball cap." He then started going through the rest of the items on the shelf.

Deidre walked up to him and put her hand on his shoulder. "Casey, these things are all yours to take home."

Casey lowered his head and then turned around. Deidre could see tears in his eyes. "Thank you. I'd like that a lot. I didn't expect to see anything here that was once mine. I thought they probably threw everything away a long time ago."

"I'll have one of the girls quickly box everything up for you, or if it would be easier for you, we can ship everything to you since you're flying home."

Casey agreed it would probably be easier if they shipped it to him. "I'll pay you back for the postage." Deidre patted him on the back and told him not to worry about it. Just before they left the room, Casey noticed his walkie-talkie sitting on the dresser next to the door. When he picked it up, he noticed it was on. Why would it be on, let alone still work? He pressed the side button and called out, "Lion to Tiger, are you there?" He laughed as he was putting it back on the dresser.

"Tiger to Lion, roger that. I don't believe these things are still working? Come to my room. I have more to show you." Cassie sounded as excited as he was.

"Roger that I'm on my way."

The first thing Casey saw when he walked into Cassie's room was her holding Betsey out to him. "Do you believe she's here? She's been here all along. And all my other toys are here along with some posters I had and all my hair accessories. They didn't throw a thing away." She looked at Deidre. "Sara said you probably wouldn't mind if I kept the things that were mine." Casey told her what Deidre told him and that she would ship everything to them. "We don't know how to thank you. I feel so bad about the way I acted toward all of you. I hope you can forgive me for all the hateful things I've said to all of you."

Sara walked up to Cassie and placed her hand on each side of Cassie's face. "I hope more than anything else that maybe this visit might have brought a little more love for your parents back into your lives."

Tears formed up in Cassie's eyes. "You have no idea how this visit has changed my whole prospective on my life here." Then she informed Deidre she'd like to take Betsey with her today. Deidre smiled and said that would be fine.

Cassie and Sara were going down the stairs when Casey stopped at the door of his parents' bedroom. Deidre followed him as he stepped in and looked around. "I always thought this room was so big when I was little. Now it looks so small. When Dad had to work in the barn until late in the night, Mom would let us get in her bed as she read to us. I can't believe that little bed is the same bed that I once thought was so big." He turned to Deidre and smiled. "I had no idea how many good memories I would have about this place. Dad was right. He gave us everything we needed. Because of our greed, we let all those happy memories fade away. If you hadn't let us come today, we may have never remembered the good things about our childhood. Thank you, Deidre." Deidre never said a word as he hugged her and then stepped out of the room.

Casey and Deidre joined the others, and Casey explained to Cassie about their parents' bedroom. Cassie handed Casey the box with the pictures, and she carried Betsey. Cassie walked up to André before they left. "I have a lot I should say, but I need to get going, so I'll just say thanks for giving me one last chance."

André smiled. "You're welcome. It's what Ben would have wanted. He would have been so happy to know the two of you came back one more time."

Deidre and Sara walked the twins to their car. As they were leaving, Deidre put her arm around Sara's shoulder, and together they watched them drive away. "Do you believe what just happened?"

Sara shook her. "Not in a million years."

CHAPTER 17

It had been a long day, so Deidre and the girls decided to come back another day to go through the house. As they were leaving, John and Daniel showed up to start clearing the field. Deidre commented to Carissa about what she had said earlier. "A little late for lunch with Daniel, isn't it?"

Carissa shrugged her shoulders. "I'm sorry for lying, but I didn't like how nosey Cassie was being. I still think at first she was trying to find out who got what. I know everything turned out for the best, but I have to tell you I'm really glad they're gone. Everyone was so uptight when they were around. Sorry, but I've got to go. I see some handsome man over there I'd like to talk to." She kissed her grandmother, and then she was off running.

Sara was talking to John as Deidre walked up to them. "Hey, John, where's the equipment you'll need to clear the land and plow it?"

John put his arm around his wife's shoulders and had the biggest grin on his face. "Right there in the barn. Yesterday Daniel and I came and checked out all the equipment that was in there. We had to do a little work on some of them, but actually everything was in pretty good condition after all these years. So were all set and ready to go."

Deidre realized all three of them were there, so she asked who was running the store.

"We have a young woman named Mary Beth who works for us part-time that is there. Sara called and said she was leaving soon, so I felt that she could handle the store by herself for a while. Besides, she ran the store all by herself the whole day we were at the lawyer's office. She starts working full-time tomorrow."

Deidre couldn't be happier for them. They both seemed so happy about the land and all the plans they had for the future. She said her good-byes and gathered the girls, and they started for the car. John yelled at them while they were leaving; "Maybe next time you come, you won't have to walk so far to get from the car to the house." Deidre and the girls waved and continued to the car.

It took a week before Deidre and the girls could work their schedules together so that the three of them could go through Ben's house. Deidre wanted to get it done so that John and Sara could start making plans for the house. Deidre called Sara to let her know when they planned on going to the house.

Sara was excited for Deidre and the girls to see everything that she, John, and Daniel had gotten done. "I think you guys will be shocked at what we've gotten done so far. John is very seldom at the store anymore, and he's worn completely out every night. But I've never seen him so happy. I'll let him know when you guys are coming. I know he'll want to be there to show you everything. I'd be there, but I'm in the middle of inventory at the store."

As they were driving there, Deidre told the girls what Sara had said. Carissa had to admit something to her. "I've already seen a lot. I've been there a few times, making lunch for them. It's the only way I can see Daniel because he has to help his dad. I have to admit I've been looking around in the house just a little. I didn't tell you about anything because they wanted to surprise you. You'll be so shocked when you see everything."

The first thing Deidre noticed was the drive going from the road to the house had been widened, and there was gravel on it now. André was sitting in the backseat. "Wow, this is nice! It's no longer scary like it was when we first came down it. What did they do? Cut down all the trees?"

Carissa explained. "Yes, but there weren't really any big trees, just a lot of small trees and really tall weeds and brush."

The road didn't stop where it used to. It continued all the way up to the house. It went all the way up next to the house. And the shed that was close to the house looked completely different. They had made it into a garage. After Deidre stopped the car, they just sat there for a moment and looked around. They were parked next to the porch. It was completely cleared off, and now a swing hung on the end of it. They could see the double windows that had once been hidden by all the stuff on the porch, which had now been cleared away.

Deidre was in complete awe of everything. "Do you believe all this?"

Carissa couldn't wait for them to see everything else. "Wait until you see everything else they've done. Every time I come here, there's something different to see."

Deidre was a little confused. "But I thought they weren't going to do anything right now except for the land."

Carissa was already out of the car and heading for the back of the house.

As Deidre and André were getting out of the car, John came walking around the shed, wiping his hands on a cloth. "Well, what do you think? It's nice to be able to drive all the way up to the house, isn't it?"

"Oh, John, it all looks so amazing. I just can't believe my eyes. You guys have done so much. Just look at that beautiful porch, and the swing looks perfect up there."

John started walking toward the porch, and Deidre with André followed him. "The swing was here all along. It was sitting on the floor of the porch with tons of stuff on top of it. All the stuff that was sitting on it must have protected it because all we had to do was replace the chains and paint the swing. It's Sara's favorite place to sit on the porch."

Deidre stepped up on the porch and walked over and sat on the swing. "I bet now that everything is gone from in front of these two windows, there's a lot more sunlight in the front room."

"Not to mention that Sara painted the living room and put up new curtains. Don't worry. She didn't touch anything of yours. She's been working around it all."

Deidre apologized for not getting back until now to go through the house. "We'll make sure to get as much done as possible so that we can get all this stuff out of your way."

John assured her it wasn't a problem. "We have so much to do everywhere that we just go where we can to work." He stopped Deidre as she was about to walk into the house. "Before you go inside, I'd like to show you the rest of what we did outside—if you don't mind and if you have the time."

"Sure, I'd love to see everything you've done, and we have plenty of time. Don't we, André?"

Andre smiled. "Nothing but time."

John led them to the back of the house, where Carissa joined Daniel. Deidre gasped. "It's beautiful. Everything is gone. You can see the creek perfectly. Wow, you even fixed and painted the pigsty and chicken coops! But I don't understand why. Are you planning to have some pigs and chickens?" Then she noticed that the outhouse had been fixed and painted. "Don't tell me you're going to use the outhouse."

John snickered as he answered her question. "First of all, no, we're not going to use the outhouse as a bathroom. I'm really hoping to keep as much of the original farm as I can. I gutted the outhouse and filled the hole. We're storing things in it now. As for the chickens and pigs, you just never know." He looked at both of their feet. "Good you have tennis shoes on this time. Let me show you the field on the other side of the barn."

Carissa and Daniel joined them as they walked around to the other side of the barn. Carissa didn't wait for Deidre to say something. "Isn't it amazing what they've done? And look how far the land goes." You could tell that Carissa was very proud of her fiancé.

Deidre was taking it all in. She now could see the farm as it once was. "Are those two silos way over there?"

John told her about them. "Yes, they are. They need some work done on them, but I think they'll be usable someday. Ben had a very self-sufficient farm here. You have to realize that besides all this land, he also had land on the other side of those silos that he sold years ago … and then the land on the other side of the creek. Once Ben's brothers were no longer a part of the farm and it was just him working it, that's when he no longer worked all the land on the other side of the creek. To tell you the truth, I have no idea how he did it all by himself."

Deidre watched John as he was talking, and she could tell how much he loved the farm and the history of it.

"Well, I know the three of you have a lot to go through in the house, so I'll let you get to it. Daniel and I are working on the inside of the shed, which as you have seen, will now be our garage. I don't know if Sara told you, but we're hoping to move in by fall."

The news didn't surprise Deidre, but she was surprised that they were planning for so soon. "That's great! What all are you planning on doing before you move in?"

John explained, "We're having a new roof put on and a new furnace put in. We're replacing all the windows, and naturally there's a lot of painting. The rest will have to wait until next year."

As Deidre and the girls were walking back to the house, Carissa entwined her arm around Deidre's arm. "Wait till you see the inside of the house. They've done so much to the kitchen. Actually it was Sara that did the work, but—" Carissa stopped but then continued, "I'm not saying anymore because I don't what to spoil the surprise."

When Deidre walked into the house, she was more than surprised. Carissa walked in before Deidre and André. She turned around so that she could see their expressions. "Isn't it nice and bright? There are new curtains, but that's all they could do for now because of all the stuff. They've been doing some rewiring of some kind." It just didn't seem like the same house. Then Deidre noticed that Ben's picture was hanging over the fireplace. It had been placed in a larger frame. She looked over at Carissa with a puzzled look.

"Sara loved that picture, and I thought that if I gave her the picture to hang in the house, it would be a way for Ben to still be a part of the house. I had no idea she was going to hang it over the fireplace. I helped her pick out a larger frame so that it would be in proportion of the fireplace. They're planning to have the fireplace redone sometime."

André walked up to it and put her hand on the picture. "I miss him so much." Deidre seconded the comment.

Carissa brought their focus back to the house. "Wait until you see the kitchen! That's where you're really going to be shocked." As before, Carissa walked in front of them so that she could see their expressions when they saw the kitchen.

What had once been a simple kitchen was now an up-to-date modern kitchen. There was a new floor and cabinets with countertops along with all new appliances. They had painted the kitchen and had new curtains. "How did they have the time to do all this along with all the work they did outside?"

Carissa sat down at the old table and chairs that they had left for Deidre. "They had all this done by professionals. Except Sara painted and put up the curtains." Then she got up and walked up to the new sink.

"Come look out the window. You can see all the way to the creek now that they cleared all the land."

Deidre looked out the window and remembered all the stories that Casey and Cassie had shared with them about their childhood. She could imagine Annie looking out this window, watching her children play. She stood there so long that André stepped up next to her to see if she was all right. Deidre smiled over at André as she put her arm around her. "I was just daydreaming for a minute about how it might have been back when this house and farm was alive with a family living in it. And now it's starting to come back alive again."

Deidre took a big breath and turned around. "Well, let's start digging into all this stuff and get it done so this family can finish transforming this house into a home."

Carissa showed Deidre the boxes of stuff that Sara had packed up to ship to the twins. "She didn't what to ship it until you had a chance to go through it and okay everything."

Deidre didn't bother with going through the boxes. "There's no need to do that. I'm sure Sara knew what belonged to them. We might end up adding more to them before we're done."

Some boxes of items were in the kitchen. Cassie explained what Sara had done with those boxes. "Sara divided up things that were broken or just junk from the things we may want."

Each of them took a box to go through. Carissa kept a lot of things for when she and Daniel got married. André didn't really need anything from the kitchen, and Deidre had everything she needed for a kitchen. She did like a few of the really old items. They were quickly done with the kitchen items, and they agreed that no one wanted the table and chairs. But Deidre wanted the old wooden hutch.

No one wanted most of the living room furniture, but Deidre wanted the linen chest and the large curio cabinet that had once been in the corner. But she wondered about the items that had once been inside. Since Sara painted the room, they assumed she must have packed them in one of the boxes. André was the one who found the box. "Oh, Grandma! You need to see this. It must be what we're looking for. There are some beautiful glass things in it and some figurines." They went through it and decided to keep it all. Deidre noticed that André had an eye for antiques. Deidre knew there must be more items somewhere, and at that moment Carissa found two more boxes next to each other. Those had even more items that were very old and beautiful.

As they were going through the boxes, André asked her grandmother, "How old do you think these item are, Grandma?

Deidre told her they were probably a few generations old. They decided to take the boxes home and finish going through them later.

There were quite a few smaller items in the living room that each of them wanted, and then there were a few items that Deidre knew were antiques. She told the girls she would have the items appraised. She would sell what they didn't want to keep and split the money between the three of them. Once they were done with the downstairs, they went upstairs to the bedrooms. There was nothing in the twins' rooms that any of them wanted, so they went straight to Ben and Annie's room. André fell in love with a vanity set that had belonged to Annie. "Look at this old mirror, comb, and brush set, Grandma. Isn't it beautiful? And oh, look at these hair barrettes. Do you think Ben kept them here to remind him of Annie? It looks like he made sure they were kept clean." It was obvious to Deidre that André wanted them.

Deidre was surprised when Carissa was interested in the bed tables and the vanity table. Carissa had more modern tastes. Deidre fell in love with a secretarial desk and a large wooden wardrobe chest. When she opened it, she saw that Ben's clothes were still inside. The three of them stopped what they were doing to look at the clothes. Then they quietly continued going through things. André asked if she could have the quilt that was on the bed, and Deidre decided to keep the headboard.

Carissa walked up to a small closet. Like the other bedroom closets, it didn't have a door, but she couldn't find a switch. Deidre stepped up and reached up to search for a cord. She pulled down on it, and the light came on. There were only a few pieces of clothing that looked like they belonged to Annie. On the floor there was a storage chest. It was so heavy that it took both Carissa and Deidre to pull it out. They pulled it over toward the bed, and Deidre and André sat on the bed while Carissa opened it. When Carissa opened the chest, it took a minute before any of them knew what they were looking at.

André went from the bed to the floor next to Carissa. She reached down and carefully brought out a wedding dress that was in a clear bag. She slowly stood up and lifted the dress out. Deidre and Carissa stood up as André laid the dress on the bed. André slowly and gently took the plastic off the dress. "It must be Annie's wedding dress." By the look of the dress, Deidre expressed that it was probably handed down to Annie by her mother.

The dress was satin with pearls scattered on the upper part, and there was lace on top of satin on the body and skirt parts. The sleeves were also satin with tiny button spanning from the elbow to the wrist. There were also tiny buttons that went down the back. As they were looking, Carissa looked into the chest again. "I wonder where the veil is."

André never took her eyes off the dress as Deidre guessed. "Maybe it was used for something, Cassie. Veils aren't normally handed down, just the dresses"

While she was still holding the dress, André turned to Carissa. "You should have this cleaned and altered so that you can wear it for your wedding."

Carissa was caught off guard. "Uh, I don't know about that André. That's just not my taste."

André was shocked that Carissa didn't jump at the chance to wear it. "You haven't even tried it on, and like I said, you can alter it and make some changes to it."

Carissa didn't really think she wanted to do that, so she ended the conversation; "We'll take it with us and look into it."

As the two of them were discussing the wedding dress, Deidre was looking to see what else was in the chest. Her heart melted when she realized it was filled with Annie's personal items. André laid the dress across the bed and joined the other two as they started going through the chest. There was a small music box with a locket inside that had Annie's name on it and a picture of who they guessed was Annie when she was little with another little girl. There were some pictures in frames that they guessed showed Annie's family. They found a few necklaces and a couple of white gloves and some elegant handkerchiefs. André opened a box and found old love letters that Ben had written to Annie when he was away in the military, and Deidre found Annie's love letters to Ben. Carissa found an old picture album that was coming apart. It was filled with lots of very old pictures. There were a few other odds and ends, and then at the bottom of the chest, there were two baby books. One belonged to Casey, and the other one belonged to Cassie. Deidre wondered about the other items. "Maybe we should ask Casey and Cassie if they would like to go through all their parents' personal items and see if there's anything they might like."

Carissa agreed, but André was hesitant. "Even the wedding dress?"

Deidre told her it would only be fair. "I can see us keeping home decor items and furniture, but these things are personal things that belonged to their parents."

André wasn't sure she agreed. "Is the vanity set considered a personal item?" Carissa told her yes, but she thought André should be able to keep it.

Deidre told the two of them what she would say to Casey and Cassie. "I'll tell them what we found in the chest, and then I'll ask them if there is anything else in the house that is personal that they remembered and would like to have."

André wasn't really happy about it, but she agreed with her grandmother's plans. She quietly commented, "Ben said everything in the house belonged to us. I would think this is part of that." Deidre didn't comment.

Carissa started laughing when she looked in the nightstand. "Look what Ben had in his nightstand?" She showed them the picture and the article about him and the art showing that appeared in the paper. The three of them laughed as they looked at it.

André looked at it longer than the other two. "You don't think he was very proud of that moment, do you? Can I have this? I didn't save a copy for myself." Carissa told her sure. She had three or four copies anyway. "But this is the one that Ben kept, so I'd really like to have it."

The time had come for them to go up into the attic. There was a door at the end of the hall that opened up to stairs that led to the attic. There was no switch at the bottom, so Deidre knew they would have to climb the stairs and find the switch at the top of the stairs. Carissa decided to go get a flashlight from the kitchen. When she got back, Deidre had already gone up the stairs and found the light. Carissa looked at André. "After you."

André motioned to the stairs. "No, after you. I'm the scaredy-cat, remember?"

Deidre yelled at both of them. "Good grief. It's not that bad. It's a little dirty, but that's all. Quit playing around and get up here so we can get this done." The two girls looked at each other, and Carissa gave in and went up first.

The attic was packed solid with furniture and boxes. Deidre was trying to make her way to some windows that were covered with newspaper. When she tore the paper off, she realized the windows had latches. It took some work to get them open, but once she did, it really helped get a breeze blowing through it and clear away some of the musty smell. It also brought in more light. The three of them looked around to see where they wanted to start.

Deidre couldn't believe all the antiques up there. André found an old windup phonograph, and at the same time, Carissa found an old radio in a wooden case. As they continued to look, Carissa found an old artist easel and an old box next to it. When she opened it, she found artist supplies. Most of it was no longer any good, but she loved the idea that someone who once lived there had been an artist. There were boxes of clothes, old toys, and lots of papers. One of the boxes that Deidre opened had some papers that caught her eye. It was the original deed to the land and the boundaries to the original property. She decided that maybe John would like to have this information. As a matter of fact, he would probably like to go through all the boxes of papers. There was a lot of history in them.

André took Deidre's attention off what she was going through. "Grandma, Carissa, come here." André was in the corner of the attic, just standing and looking at something. When the two of them got to her, Deidre realized that the attic had once been a bedroom. That part of the room was a baby's room. There was another set of windows. Deidre made her way to them, tore the papers off, and got the windows opened. They could now see so much more on this end of the attic.

You could tell more clearly that it was once a living quarters and not just items stored up there. It was almost like someone didn't want items stored in that area to keep it the way it once was. There was a crib, a rocking chair, a dresser, and a table with a lamp on it. There was a rug next to the crib. There was a blue baby blanket lying over the side of the bed that was covered in dust. When she saw this part of the room, Deidre started looking around the attic in more detail. Besides a baby's room, there was also a bedroom and an area that was like a sitting room. She turned to the girls. "This was once another part of the house." She pointed to an area. "Over there is a bedroom, and if you'll look across to over there, that's an area they used as a sitting room."

André looked puzzled. "You mean like another family lived up here besides the family that lived downstairs?"

Deidre explained as much as she had heard once. "Back years ago family members would get married but still remain living at home." Deidre thought that probably somewhere in those boxes of papers was the information on all the people who had lived there once.

André felt there was something more to it. "But Grandma, wouldn't they have changed the baby's area into a child's area with time. And look how everything is placed a certain way. I think maybe the baby died." Carissa agreed that André might be right.

As Carissa and Deidre continued to go through piles of things, André remained in the baby's room. Deidre came back to her. "Honey, you have to let go of it, and let's finish what we came here to do."

André was sitting in the rocking chair, holding the baby blanket. "I wonder what his name was and how long he lived before he died."

Deidre knelt down in front of her and put her hands on André's knees. "After John gets a chance to go through all the boxes of papers, I'll bet he'll know all about it, and I'll ask him if he'll call and let us know once he does, okay?"

André loved the way her grandmother always tried to understand how she felt and didn't just brush things off. "I'd like that." She placed the blanket back where she had found it and joined the other two.

The things they found in the attic weren't what one would expect a farm family to own. From the look of a lot of these things, someone had money.

There was a beautiful jeweled jewelry box that stored some gorgeous pieces of jewelry. There was one cedar chest that had some very beautiful women's clothing that looked like they were very expensive in their time. Then there was another cedar chest with women's accessories that you would never see on a farm. There was a man's wardrobe valet stand and also a man's barber vanity. Deidre uncovered a long full-length mirror with legs and had two drawers on the bottom. They found many jeweled trinket boxes and music boxes along with figurines. It made no sense to Deidre why those things were in the attic.

They had finally gone through everything, but now they had to make plans for how to get everything down out of the attic. There was no way Deidre and the girls could do it by themselves. There were so many boxes and so much furniture. Deidre was going to go through everything with John and Sara, and then she planned on renting a storage space to store all the items they were keeping.

When they got down to the main floor, they found Sara in the kitchen, making dinner. "I was going to have to bring dinner to John and Daniel, so I decided I'd just make dinner here so that you guys could have something to eat too."

Before Deidre had a chance to say anything, Carissa was thanking Sara. "Thanks. We're starving. We've been here all day, and we skipped lunch. I didn't realize how hungry I was until I smelled the food."

André stepped up to Sara and volunteered to help her. Sara took her up on the offer and had her start on the salad.

Deidre set the table, and Carissa went to go get John and Daniel. During dinner Deidre told the Matthews what they had found in the attic. She told John about all the papers and how she thought he'd find out a lot about the history of the house and land. Then she told them about the items and how there must have been someone living there who once had money.

John told her what he had heard when he was younger. "Ben had an uncle who married a woman who was from a wealthy family. The story went that she was pregnant when they got married and that her father disowned her."

André spoke quietly as she asked, "Did the baby die?"

John was surprised that she had asked. "Why, yes, it did. It was a boy, and he died from phenomena when he was four months old. How did you know?"

"The nursery is in the attic, and it looks like it was left the way it was when the baby was alive—except for the fact that everything is so dusty and dirty." André looked down at her food as she asked, "Do you know what the baby's name was?" John told her that he didn't know any of their names.

André asked another question before Deidre had a chance to continue talking to John. "What happened to the woman who had the baby? Did she die too?" Deidre was wondering why André was asking all of these questions.

But John was intrigued with all the questions. "As matter of fact, she did. But not for a couple of years after the baby died. A year after her baby died, she became pregnant again but had a miscarriage when the baby was five months along. She hardly ever left the attic after that. Her husband found her in their bed. She had committed suicide there by cutting her wrist."

Everyone was quiet for some time before André said, "I guess she wanted to be with her babies."

After dinner John, Sara, and Deidre walked through the house and the attic, and Deidre told them about everything they were planning to have picked up. "Let me know what you don't want, and I'll have it all hauled away."

John volunteered his services to Deidre and the girls. "Don't worry about hauling anything away. I have a large hauling truck that we'll use. I can move your stuff for you as well. Just let me know when and where."

Deidre was so happy that John could help her out. "Why don't I call you and make arrangements so that Brad, Taylor, and Ryan can be here to help?" John agreed that would work.

When they were about to leave, André came down the stairs with a box that she had packed with some of the things she wanted. "I thought I'd take some of the things with me now. I only have this one box."

Daniel took the box for her to the car. "It may be only one box, but it must be packed to its fullest because it's really heavy."

They said their good-byes, but this time Deidre knew it wasn't the last time she'd see the place. She knew she'd at least see it one more time.

CHAPTER 18

It took a week for everyone to get together to pack everything up at Ben's house. There were so many people helping that Deidre felt it wouldn't take any time at all to pack things up. Deidre and Brad along with Carissa came early because Carissa wanted her grandmother to see once again how much had been done. She was right! As they were driving up to the house, Deidre couldn't believe how different it all looked. They had put shutters on each of the window. Once they got closer, she realized that the house had been painted.

As they walked up to the house, they saw John and Sara sitting on the porch, drinking their morning coffee. Sara asked if they would like a cup. Brad accepted, but Deidre had already had enough coffee for the day.

Brad went on and on about how great everything looked. "I remember that day when we all came out here to work. Even with all the work we did, it didn't come anywhere near how it looks now." After Sara brought Brad some coffee, John asked Brad if he'd like to look around.

Sara shook her head. "John, let Brad sit and drink his coffee first." She looked over at Deidre. "Every time anyone comes around, he just has to show them everything. He's so proud of this place and what he and Daniel have done."

Deidre had to admit she didn't blame him. Sara confessed that they had received some help a couple of times from some church friends. "A group of men came out and helped with clearing the woods and helped with the gravel up to the house. One day they surprised John and showed up to help paint the barn and clear the field for planting. They cut down a lot of trees way over where the silos are. They also came and helped clear things away behind the house. Every time John talks about all the work that he's done, he never mentions the help he gets, and that really upsets me. We talked about it the other night, and he agreed I was right and said he'd change that, so we'll see what he tells Brad."

Deidre laughed because she knew what that was like. "There have been times when Brad and I would get a lot done around our house, but when he would talk about it to others, you'd think he did it all by himself."

They both laughed, and Sara then asked Deidre to come in and look around at some of the changes. "We didn't really change a lot, but we did get rid of a lot. We also boxed up everything for you."

"You didn't have to box everything up. Taylor is bringing tons of boxes."

Sara assured her it wasn't a problem. "We were boxing everything that you left to us, so we just continued to box your things as well. But if you don't mind, we could use some of those boxes that your son is bringing." Deidre told her she could have all she wanted.

When Deidre walked in the house, she had mixed emotions about how everything looked. All of Ben's things were gone except for what Deidre was taking. It no longer looked like Ben's place. "Oh, wow, this room looks so much bigger!" She wondered if Sara was going to use any of Ben's furniture. "Was there anything of Ben's things that you're keeping, or are you planning to sell it all?"

Sara could hear in Deidre's voice a kind of sadness. "As a matter of fact, I'm keeping quite a few items. I'm having a professional restore a few things. The end tables and coffee tables were very old, so they were worth the money to have restored, and there was also a floor lamp that was an antique that I'm having redone. Upstairs we've kept some of the dressers and Cassie's headboard. We boxed up some things that we're going to use because we're having the carpet pulled up. You wouldn't believe this, but there are beautiful hardwood floors under this carpet." She walked Deidre over to where they had pulled the carpet up in the corner. "Tomorrow some professionals are coming in to redo the fireplace, and there's some work that has to be done to the chimney." They started walking back to the porch as Sara added, "If there's anything that you've changed your mind on and you want, you're more than welcome to have it."

Deidre assured her that she had everything she wanted. As they stepped out onto the porch, they saw that everyone else had arrived along with Marie and Serena. Serena ran up to hug her grandmother. "I didn't want to come, but Mom made me. I wanted to stay with my friend Katie, but Mom said you needed all the help you could get. So here I am. What do you want me to do?"

Deidre smiled at Sara and then at Serena. "We'll get everyone together and get started shortly." She remembered how Ben called Serena Spitfire. Boy did that name fit her perfectly.

Everything was going as quickly as Deidre had expected. Upstairs the twins' rooms were already bare. They had painted the walls, and the floors had been redone. They had put doors on the closets, and new curtains were up. Ben and Annie's room hadn't been touched yet. Sara explained that her sister and brother in-law came over one day and helped. Before they went into the attic, Sara wanted to speak to Deidre. "We didn't touch anything in the attic except to take the boxes of papers that you showed John. He couldn't wait to start going through them. Everything was so packed up there that we didn't feel you had a chance to really go through everything, but once a lot of the stuff is out of there, you'll be able to see better. Speaking of the attic, John found out the names of the couple that lived upstairs and the name of the baby that died. They were Michael and Sandra Crawford, and the baby's name was Daniel. John plans on telling André today."

Deidre knew John would find out a lot of information about the house and the family that lived here. "I bet there was a lot of history in those boxes. I knew John would be the one to appreciate it the most." Sara was right. There were a lot more things in the attic that they had not seen the first time. She was glad that they had a second chance to go through everything.

They found another chest that was a lot bigger than the others. When they opened it, they found all kinds of sterling silver items. Marie helped her mother go through it, and they found candleholders, silverware, silver planters, bowls, and a tea set. There were a number of frames and other things. Brad told them they would have to remove some or all the items because the chest itself was going to be so heavy that it would be hard to move. So they started boxing things up. When they got to the bottom, Marie found a silver box with small stones on it. She was shocked when she opened it. "Whoa, Mom, I think you need to see this." As she handed it to her mother, she asked, "Do you think they're real?"

They both stood up as Deidre brought out each piece of diamond jewelry to look at and then handed them to Marie to hold. There was a necklace that was designed to look like lace but was made up of small diamonds. Then there was a bracelet that had two rows of small diamonds all the way around it. There was a pair of earrings that dangled down with five small diamonds on each. Last was a round diamond ring that had two rows of small diamonds, and in the middle there was a medium blue stone. Marie was looking at the ring with her mother. "Is that a blue topaz in the middle?"

"No, dear, I believe that's a blue diamond." Deidre couldn't take her eyes off the ring because it was so beautiful.

When they put the jewelry back into the silver box, Marie asked her mother again, "So you do think they're real? What about the stones on the box? Do you think they're real too?"

Deidre looked at the stones on the box and then up at her daughter. "I'm not sure, but I believe they are. I'll need a jeweler to examine all of these to confirm that they're real and give me a value on them."

Marie was so excited for her mother. She gave her a high five. "Way to go, Mom. I think you just hit the mother lode. Whoa!" Deidre chuckled and told her to take the box to her car while she continued to go through the attic.

Deidre had found so many things that she decided to keep. André came up to her and shared with her what John had told her about the family that lived up there once. Deidre didn't let on that she knew. "I'm glad he found out for you. Does it make you feel better?"

"Yes, but it's still a sad story. He said Sandra was from a very wealthy family and that after her father died, she still didn't go back home. So her mother shipped a lot of things to her. I guess she didn't want to leave her baby. John found out there's a family grave site on the property. It's somewhere on the other side of the woods down the road. I think once he finds it, I might come back to see it." André had always been an oversensitive person. That was a trait that Deidre loved about her.

Sara and Carissa had made lunch for everyone. Some ate inside, and some ate outdoors. Deidre decided to eat outdoors. She sat in Ben's rocker, which she told Sara to keep. "It just wouldn't be right to take this rocker off the porch." Sara agreed and thanked her for letting them keep it.

André sat on the steps to eat. "This is like having a picnic. Ben and Annie would have liked this. Remember when Ben told us how much Annie loved picnics?" André talked a lot about Ben.

It took a few more hours to get the rest of the items packed. The guys had a lot of trouble getting the furniture that Deidre wanted down from the attic, but she was so pleased with how they took extra care not to damage anything. The girls brought down all the smaller things and the boxes they had packed.

It took a lot longer to pack everything up than they had hoped. So Brad and John decided that it would be better to wait until the next day to take it and unload it into the storage place that they had rented. "John, I have Taylor and Ryan plus a couple of other guys I know who can unload all this tomorrow after church. So if you don't mind, I can take your truck, and we can probably get this done without you and Daniel. The both of you have done more than we can ever thank you for, and I know the two of you have a lot to do now that everything that the girls want is out of the house."

John made sure that Brad didn't need their help and then told him he was more than happy to let them take the truck. Brad made arrangements for returning the truck. "I know you'll need the truck, so we'll make sure we get the truck back to you by tomorrow evening." John agreed he would need it and thanked Brad.

Deidre was glad that she had labeled the boxes. That way they could take certain boxes to her house and go through the stuff first. She knew there was a lot for her and the girls to go through. Then there was finding professionals to tell her the value of each item and people who wanted to buy the things they didn't want to keep. It was going to take some time to get it all done.

It had been five days since they had moved everything out of Ben's house. Deidre and André were going through some more boxes when Carissa showed up. Deidre thought she had class and was working that day. She was about to say that to her when she saw her red eyes and tear-streaked face. Carissa just stood there, trying to say something but trying not to cry at the same time. The first thing Deidre thought was that she and Daniel had broken up. She stood up from the chair she was sitting in and stepped over some boxes to get to her. "Carissa, what's wrong? What's happened?"

It was hard to understand what she was trying to say at first because she started crying as she was trying to talk. Deidre put her arm around her to try to calm her down. "Honey, I can't understand a word that you're saying. Please come and sit down and take your time."

As Carissa sat down, André handed her a glass of water, and the two of them sat down on each side of her. Carissa took a sip of water and then took a deep breath. "There was a fire." She started to get chocked up again. Deidre asked her where. Carissa took another deep breath. "Ben's house." As Deidre and André looked at each other, Carissa continued in a slightly calmer voice. "Late last night the house and the shed next to it that they had made into a garage burned to the ground. There's nothing left except the fireplace and foundation." She started to get chocked up again but regained her composer. "The garden is all gone, and the tree with the tree house is gone along with some of the trees in front of the house. No one was there to report the fire, so the firemen didn't get there until it was too late." She looked back and forth from Deidre to André. "It's all gone—all the work they did and all the money they put into it. It's all gone." She was crying again, and André had tears in her eyes.

Deidre was in complete shock. "Do you know if they got out the rest of the things that were in the house?"

Carissa told her yes. "The house was empty, and the fireplace had just been repaired and refinished."

André asked if they knew what started it. Carissa told them what Daniel had told her. "A fire inspector is going to investigate it and let them know for sure what and where it started, but Daniel said his father thinks it was an electrical fire."

That surprised Deidre. "I thought a professional electrician did the work for them. If so, then they're liable."

Carissa just shook her head. "I don't know about all that. I just know Sara is so hurt and brokenhearted. Naturally John wants the inspection done as soon as possible so that he can have the insurance company come look at everything, and then he wants to start clearing the debris away as soon as possible. You know how John is always in a hurry. Daniel said he can tell how upset his father is by the way he's running around like a chicken with his head cut off. I'm not quite sure what that means, but that's what he said."

Deidre called Sara the following morning. When Sara answered the phone, you could hear the sadness in her voice. "Hi, Sara. This is Deidre. Carissa told us yesterday about the fire. I can't tell you how sorry I am and how heartbroken we all are for you guys. Have you any idea yet about what might have caused the fire?"

Sara thanked her for her concern and added, "I was about to call you. Is there any way you can come out to the house today? I guess I mean the property … now that there's no house any longer. There's something I'd like to show you. I'd tell you on the phone, but I'd rather you came out and saw it for yourself." Deidre asked when she should come, and Sara responded, "As soon as possible, if you don't mind." Deidre told her she could be there in about an hour.

It broke Deidre's heart when she drove up and saw all the debris that was left from the fire. She sat in her car for a moment, looking at it all. When she got out of the car, she could see that the flower garden had been completely destroyed. The trees where she was parked were black and charred. John and Sara came walking from the barn, holding hands. He heart ached for them.

She hugged each of them and made sure to fight off the tears for their sake. "What can I say except I'm so sorry this happened to you?"

You could tell it was hard for Sara to talk, so she let John do the talking. "We can build another house, but it won't have the history that this house had. That's what we loved the most about the house, its history." Deidre nodded her head in understanding. "The garden will take some time, and the trees that were burnt will have to be cut down. But in time it will all be beautiful again just in a different way." John knew Sara was at the verge of tears, so he put his arm around her. "It didn't take any time at all for the fire inspector to find out the cause of the fire. I thought it was an electrical fire, but it wasn't. It was arson." Deidre gasped with shock. "According to the inspector, whoever did it first vandalized the property and then as an afterthought decided to torch the house. He said he could tell because the glass from the windows on the first floor was laying inside, which indicated they were all broken from the outside. If the broken glass from the windows was lying outside, that would have happened because of the fire. There were other signs too like all the statues in the garden were broken. We thought maybe the fire caused an explosion and broke them, but the inspector said that they were too far away for that to happen. They've declared that the fire was caused by arson after the vandalism."

Deidre couldn't believe what she was hearing. "Why on earth would someone want to do a thing like this?"

John shared the inspector's speculation. "It was probably teenagers or a gang of some sort. The fire inspector said they will need more time to investigate the fire to see if they can come up with some kind of evidence that might lead them to whoever might have done it. That means we can't do anything until they're done with their investigation. We can't even file anything with our insurance company, even though I did contact them and let them know what was up."

Sara spoke up, "There's more. That's why we wanted you to come out here."

Deidre couldn't believe there could possibly be more. Sara started walking into the woods toward Ben's and Annie's grave site. She couldn't imagine the fire getting all the way out there. She didn't ask any questions. She just continued to follow Sara, John following after her.

When they reached the grave site, Deidre grabbed her mouth with both hands. "Oh no, no, no! How on earth could anyone be so heartless?" Both stones had been broken to pieces. Ben's grave was relatively fresh, but it looked like the perpetrators had tried to dig up his remains; however, they must have given up or had second thoughts. They spray-painted on each of the graves, Annie's said, "Yeah, she's dead," and Ben's said, "Dead and gone forever." There was beer bottles scattered everywhere.

Sara explained how it was discovered. "I was so upset, so I decided to come out here and sit for a while and tell Ben and Annie what had happened. I barely remember seeing everything before I passed out. The next thing I remember is hearing Daniel calling my name and yelling for John."

John continued the story, "Daniel saw Sara walking this way and didn't want her to be alone, so he decided to come and be with her. She wasn't out for long, but it sure scared Daniel. He started yelling for me at the top of his voice. When I got here, Sara had already come to. When she looked at the graves, she started bawling her eyes out. I don't think I've seen her cry so hard."

Deidre went up to Sara and held her. "Oh, Sara, you poor thing. I can't imagine how horrible that was." Sara started weeping again, so Deidre held her tighter.

Sara took a breath so that she could stop crying. "John is going to make new headstones, and we have more cherubs in the store. We'll have all this cleaned up by the end of the day. I just thought you needed to know all this, and I didn't think it would be right to tell you all this over the phone."

Deidre thanked her, and John suggested they not stay any longer. "There's no reason to continue looking at this the way it is, so let's leave. It'll look better in a couple of days."

On the way home Deidre was trying to think of a way to tell André all this. She imagined Daniel would be telling Carissa. It was all so sad.

CHAPTER 19

Over the next couple of weeks, Sara called Deidre about every day to keep her up on what was happening. Sometimes nothing had changed, but Sara would call just to talk. Deidre had an early shooting one day, so she told Sara she wouldn't be home until later that day. When the phone rang, she thought Sara had forgotten what she had told her. "Hi, is this Deidre?"

Deidre was surprised to hear Mark Talbot's voice. "Hi, Deidre, this is Mark Talbot. How are you?" After the formalities Mark told her why he was calling. "Is there any way you could come to my office sometime this week?"

Deidre was concerned that there might have been a problem with the inheritance, but that didn't make sense. "Is there anything I should be concerned about?"

Mark assured her everything was fine. "It's something totally different. If you have time, I can go over it briefly right now."

Deidre explained, "Actually I was just about to go out the door to do a shoot, so I really don't have the time right now to talk."

Mark quickly made arrangements to meet with her in two days at his office. "Maybe we'll have a chance to catch up on what's been going on with all of you since the reading of Ben's will."

Deidre wondered if he knew anything about the fire and vandalism. "That would be nice. A lot has happened. Well, I really need to go. I don't want to make my clients wait. I'll see you in a couple of days." They said their good-byes and ended the call.

It was hard for Deidre to keep focused during the shoot because she kept thinking about the conversation with Mark. "What could he want to talk to me about?" Even though he sounded like it wasn't anything for her to be concerned about, she still didn't like the feeling she had.

When she talked to Sara that afternoon, she didn't mention Mark calling. She didn't want to worry her, and she wouldn't have been able to answer any of the questions she might have asked. A couple of hours later, Sara called Deidre back. Sara was talking so fast that Deidre couldn't understand what she was saying. All she knew was Sara was saying something about the house.

Deidre had to talk really loud to get Sara's attention. "Sara! Sara! You have to slow down! I can't understand a word you're saying." Sara stopped talking. "Now what were you saying about the house?"

Deidre could hear Sara trying to pace her words so that she wouldn't ramble too fast. "They caught the guys who started the fire and vandalized the grave site." She had Deidre's complete attention. "I can't believe they caught them, let alone how fast they caught them. The police said that one of them had cut themselves somehow and that it must have been rather bad because there was quite a bit of blood. They found his blood on that big stone by Ben and Annie's graves. They checked all the immediate care sites and hospitals nearby and ran a DNA test. The guy had a criminal record, so they found him and the other four guys who were with him. Another guy had burned himself bad enough that he had to go to the hospital for treatment. I can't believe they were injured but still wanted to demolish the grave site. You'd think they would have left immediately since two of them were injured. Anyway, now they're caught. The fire inspector is finished with everything, and the insurance has settled up, so I guess we're ready to start over. John has already made plans for the cleanup.

It was good to hear the excitement in Sara's voice. "Are you and John planning on doing a lot of the work yourself, or are you going to hire it out?"

Sara's voice changed to a more serious tone. "I wish John would hire it all out, but he said it costs too much, so we're doing both. We're hiring the big stuff out, and the rest we're doing ourselves. Same with the house when we start building, so we have a long and busy summer ahead of us. We're so blessed to have friends and church family that all want to help."

Deidre volunteered her family. "You know we want to be a part of everything, so please let us know when you need us." Sara assured her that they would.

Deidre only told Brad about the phone call from Mark. "Did he want all three of you girls to come to his office or just you?" She told him just her. "But he said it didn't have anything to do with your inheritance?" She told him that was correct. "I agree it sounds strange, but I really don't think you have anything to worry about. But if you don't mind, why don't I plan on going with you?"

Deidre was so relieved. "That would be great! It's tomorrow at nine thirty in the morning. Can you get away from work okay?"

Brad told her that wouldn't be a problem. "We can make a day of it. After we leave the lawyer's office, we can head over to Richmond and then Centerville and hit some antique shops and see what they think of the pictures you took of your antique furniture. From there we'll drive home on US 40 and find somewhere to have dinner." She told him it all sounded very nice. "Then it's a date." Brad always had a way of making her feel better.

Deidre was so nervous and anxious while she was sitting in the waiting room of the law office that she just couldn't sit, so she started pacing. "Why is it taking so long? He said nine thirty, and it's close to ten o'clock now. It's just wrong to make a person wait that long."

Brad wasn't sure he could say anything that would calm Deidre down. "Doctors do it all the time. Besides, remember the day all of you were here for the reading of the will? The lawyer had to actually postpone some of his other appointments because things were taking a lot more time than he had planned. You just have to realize that things happen that are out of his control."

Deidre sat down next to him and put her hand on his knee. "You're right. It's just the not knowing why he wants to talk to me that's driving me crazy."

Finally Mark stepped out of his office and greeted them. Deidre was expecting someone to walk out of his office with him, someone who had been with him all that time. Deidre introduced Brad to Mark, and then the three of them entered his office.

There was a gentleman sitting in one of the three chairs in front of Mark's desk. Mark introduced them to him. "Deidre, Brad, this is Thomas O'Neill, Thomas, this is Deidre and Brad Hugely." He then motioned for them to have a seat. "I was hoping we'd be able to talk for a while before we got down to business, but Thomas insisted on being present at this meeting, so maybe we can talk later."

Deidre was happy that they were skipping the catch-up talk because she didn't feel like talking right now. All she wanted was to know what all this leading to. "What's going on, Mark, and why is this gentleman here?"

Thomas interrupted, "Tom. Please call me Tom."

Deidre repeated back to him, "Tom." Then she looked back at Mark and repeated her question. "What's going on Mark, and why am I here?"

Mark explained first who Thomas was. "Mr. O'Neill owns the property that is next to John and Sara Matthew's property."

Deidre jumped in, "The land that used to belong to Ben once?"

Mark was surprised that Deidre knew anything about that property.

Tom answered, "That's correct. He sold it to me many years ago."

Mark continued, "Mr. O'Neill came to me after he heard Ben died and wanted to know about the land that is located on the other side of the creek between the two farms. I told him it had been willed to someone, and since then, he has been interested in finding out about it. I was ... well, we were wondering if you've had any thought about what you might want to do with it."

Before Mark could go any further, Tom explained more in detail why he was interested. "I used to lease the two pieces of land on each side of that piece of land that you now own. Now I own them. I would very much like to buy your piece of land to go with the two that I own."

Silence filled the room. They waited so that Deidre could take it all in. "Plus you own the land next to John and Sara?" Tom answered yes. Deidre asked, "How many acres of land do you own next to the Matthews?"

Tom wasn't sure why she was asking questions about that land. "There's eighteen acres, but what does that have to do with you selling me your land?"

Deidre looked over at Mark. "Could you give me a moment with my husband?" Mark told them they could use the conference room.

When they entered the room, Brad jumped into the conversation first. "You want to trade land with him for John, don't you?"

Deidre wasn't a bit surprised that Brad knew what she was thinking. "Yes, I do, but I own two more acres. I looked into the going price for prime farming land, so I know how much it's worth. I just don't know what he's doing with his land next to John and Sara. You may not agree, but I wanted to give the land to the Matthews, but only if I can get a decent price for my extra two acres. Between the money I inherited, the money for the antiques from the house, and now the two acres, we have plenty of money. John and Sara sank so much of their inheritance into that house, and then there was the fire. They'll never get it all back, so they've lost a lot."

Brad put his hand on her shoulder. "If you want my approval on all of this, you have it. It's your money, and like you said, we have plenty. Not to mention we weren't hurting for money in the first place. You do what you want. And by the way, I'm very proud of you."

He kissed her, and they went back into the office.

The two men stood as Deidre and Brad came in and sat down. Deidre got right to the point. "To answer your first question, Mark, yes, I've looked into the value of my property, and I considered selling it. But I wasn't in any big hurry. I thought I might think of it as an investment and sell it later for more money." Then she looked at Tom. "Mr. O'Neill, you may have something that may change my mind and sell my land now."

Tom responded, "Please call me Tom. I'm guessing what I have that you might want is the eighteen acres next to the Matthews."

Brad couldn't get over how shrewd of a businessperson his wife was turning out to be. Even after all the years he'd known her, there was always something new.

Deidre continued, "That's correct. Tell me what are you doing with that land right now."

Tom replied, "I'm farming it, but it's hard for me to get to it because it's on the other side of the creek. I live on the other side of the land I farm. I don't farm all of it, only about ten acres of it the rest are trees and overgrown land. I take it you have some kind of proposition in mind."

Deidre looked at her husband and then at Tom and took a breath before she proceeded. "I don't know how much you wanted to pay for my land, but I'm willing to trade lands with you. And I'm asking eighteen thousand dollars for the extra two acres."

Tom didn't act shocked, but he had a counteroffer. "That's a lot of money for two acres of land. How about sixteen thousand dollars and the trade?"

Deidre didn't blink an eye as she came back with her offer. "Like you said, your land has trees that will have to be removed, and some of the land will have to be cleared. My land is ready and just needs to be turned and planted. Besides it's more convenient for you."

Mark stepped in to speak to Tom. "Why don't we take some time and talk this over. We can get back with Deidre later."

While Mark was speaking, Tom never took his eyes off of Deidre. "You have a deal. We will trade lands, and I will pay you eighteen thousand dollars for the two extra acres." Tom stood up, and so did Deidre. Then they shook hands. "Do we let Mark handle it all, or do you have a lawyer you want to represent you?"

Deidre looked at Mark and then back at Tom. "I trust Mark completely, but you get to pay him." They both laughed, and Tom agreed. "Oh and by the way, the creek that is by the Matthews' land belongs to them, so the creek that runs by the land I'm trading for must come with the land. You have the creek running between your properties so that should be sufficient. Is that okay with you?" Tom chuckled as he agreed. "You're a very strong negotiator, but I agree. That's fair."

Mark told them he would write up the agreement and have it ready for them both to sign in two days—that is, if Tom had the money by then. He told him he would.

Before she left the room, Deidre told Mark that she needed to discuss something with him. Tom said his good-byes, and Brad said he needed to make some phone calls and would meet her at the car.

Mark walked back around to his chair and sat down. "So what's up, Deidre?"

Deidre explained what she planned on doing with the land. "I'm giving the land that I'm trading with Tom to John and Sara, but I'm keeping the money for myself. So I don't know how we go about doing that."

Mark had to confirm what he'd just heard. "Let me get this straight. You want to give the Matthews the land, not sell it to them?"

"That's correct, but I'm keeping the money from the extra two acres. So how do we do this?"

Mark scratched his head. "Well, for tax purposes, you can't just give the land away. You have to sell the land, even if it's for just a dollar. Can

I ask why you're doing this? Why don't you sell it to them? They have the money from their inheritance."

When Deidre started telling the story about what John and Sara had gone through, Mark stopped her. "I know all about it. I'm representing them in the case against the guys who were arrested."

She questioned him, "Did they tell you how much money and time they had already put into the house? And now they have to pay out more money to build a new house."

Mark commented, "I really don't know all the details, but you do understand that they will be getting money from the insurance company? We're also looking into retrieving some money back from the perpetrators. Plus I'm not sure that's quite fair to John. He's a very proud man, and I feel that your offer might insult him more than help him."

Deidre had to admit she hadn't thought about any of the things he had just mentioned.

Mark sat back in his chair. "I have a couple of ideas I'd like for you to think over. You could sell them the land for half the value or sell it to them for just a small lump sum. You can even sell it to them on contract since they may not have all the money right now." Mark saw that Deidre needed time to think about what he had just told her. "The Matthews are coming in next Tuesday to go over the lawsuit. Why don't you think about what I just said and get back with me before then?"

Deidre agreed and then shook his hand and thanked him. As she was walking out to the car, Brad could see by the look on her face that something had changed. "Are you okay? What happened in there? Can't you do what you want for the Matthews?"

Deidre looked at Brad for a moment before she started, "I can still do it, but Mark brought up a few things that we need to talk about before I make my final decision."

The evening before Deidre was to go to Mark's office, she sat on her patio in the cool evening air with a glass of wine, thinking about everything that had happened over the past week. It was all a little overwhelming—the incident at John and Sara's place, the land deal with Mr. O'Neill, and everything else. She had connected with an antique actioner to sell their antiques, and she had set up five upcoming shootings. She laughed when she thought about talking to André the night before and asking if she could help her with the shootings. Ben had mentioned how André could help her more in his will.

Her thoughts were interrupted when Brad stepped out with a glass of wine and joined her. When she smiled at him, he could tell she was tired. "You've been one busy lady lately. Are you doing okay?" She nodded yes as she looked out at the water. "You look like you have something on your mind that you'd like to talk about?"

She turned to him and smiled. "You really need to get out of my head."

Brad smiled back at her. "You're expressions read like an open book. Okay, so what's up?"

Deidre hated to ask him this favor. "I know how you don't like to take off from work, and I know you just took off a day last week. Besides, I don't even know if you can with such last-minute notice, but I really wish you could go with me tomorrow."

Brad didn't show any reaction to her request. "Hmm, I think I might be able to arrange that."

Deidre was shocked by his remark. "But how can you do that on such short notice? Don't you have appointments?"

"I did until Friday when I asked Tracy to cancel all my appointment for tomorrow, and you know I don't do surgeries on Tuesdays. I thought I'd try to talk you into letting me tag along with you tomorrow."

Deidre had tears in her eyes. "Have I told you lately how much I love you?"

John smiled. "It's about time."

The drive to the law office seemed to take longer than normal. Then they were caught in a traffic jam because of a wreck. Deidre called Mark to let him know they would be a little late. He told her not to worry. He had no other appointments except for their appointment later that afternoon.

Even though it wasn't their fault that they were late, Deidre kept apologizing to Mark and Tom once they got to the office. Mark assured her that it was all right. "Really, Deidre, it's not a problem. It gave Tom and me a chance to go over a few other issues that Tom has about another situation."

The land transaction with Tom went quickly with no problems. Once Tom was gone, Mark went over the paperwork that Deidre had asked him to draw up over the phone. "You do know that the amount you came up with isn't even a third of the value of the land?"

Deidre knew that. "I know, but it's all I want for the land. Anything less may insult them and anything more may make it difficult for them."

Mark handed her the papers. "If you could read over the contract and make sure it's all right with you, then this afternoon we'll have it all ready to present to them." After the papers were signed, Mark asked them, "So what do the two of you plan to do between now and this afternoon? Surely you're not heading back to Indy?"

Brad shrugged his shoulder, but Deidre knew exactly what she wanted to do. "I'd like to show Brad the park that Ben and Annie liked, and then there's a special place I'd like to go to for lunch."

Mark looked at Brad. "Sounds like she has it all planned out."

Brad smiled. "She always does."

It was a warm, sunny day, but once they were under the trees in the park, it was nice. Brad and Deidre walked hand in hand through the park. She talked about the things Ben said when she brought him there the first time. They came to the bench that Ben had referred to as his and Annie's bench, and then they sat down. The playground was busy with children and mothers and few fathers. Deidre and Brad sat and watched the children play just like Ben and Annie had at one time.

Brad was the first to speak. "I miss the days when our children were little. As far as that goes, I even miss the days when our grandchildren were little. Boy, I just realized we're getting old."

Deidre squeezed his hand. "Older, not old."

After a while longer, Brad commented, "I'm hungry. Where are we going for lunch? If we don't want to hurry through lunch, I guess we'd better get going."

Deidre stood and reached for his hand. "It's a very special place. I think you'll like it. They serve home-cooked food." Brad liked that idea.

When they pulled up to Maggie's Diner, Deidre looked to see Brad's reaction. "Now this looks interesting. They say you can always find good food at these small-town diners. I take it you've been here before?"

"Quite a few times. It was Ben's favorite place to eat. It's been here for years but with different owners. I really think you'll like the food."

It was a great lunch, and they enjoyed not having to hurry. As they were heading back to the law office, they talked about the different scenarios they could see this afternoon.

When they got there, they saw the Matthews' car. Mark wanted to get the lawsuit meeting out of the way first before Deidre and Brad came. When they walked in, Deidre told June to let Mark know that they were there. June smiled. "As I was writing up the contact for the land deal with the Matthews, I couldn't believe what you were doing for them. With everything they're going through, this should really brighten up their day."

Deidre thanked her. "I think that's what Ben would want me to do for them."

It was about ten minutes later when June told them they could go in. When they entered the room, Mark stood up and greeted them. John and Sara turned around with complete puzzlement on both of their faces. Mark motioned for them to take a seat. Sara and John stood up. Deidre hugged Sara, and Brad shook John's hand. When they all sat down, Sara and John was hesitant at first. John asked, "I'm not sure what's going on here. Why are you two here?"

Mark went over the whole story about Deidre and Tom's transaction on their land deal, but he left out the amount of money Deidre received for the extra two acres of land. He then continued to place Deidre's offer to the Matthews. John and Sara looked at each other and asked Mark to repeat the offer. Deidre assured them that they had heard him correctly.

John was completely confused. "Why would you sell us that land for so cheap? I know how much that land is worth, and that doesn't come anywhere near its worth. We're sorry, Deidre, but we just can't accept that offer."

Deidre stopped John before he could go any further. "I received a good sum of money for the extra two acres, and then with my share of the inheritance, I feel I have more than my share. I only knew Ben for a little more than a year, and you guys knew and took care of him for years. I think Ben would love the idea of his farm being farmed once again by someone he cared about. Please let me do this for you in Ben's memory."

They debated back and forth until finally the Matthews accepted Deidre's offer. Sara started crying, and even John had a few tears in his eyes. They finished the paperwork and said good-bye to Mark as the four of them left the office. They talked for more than an hour in the parking lot, and then John and Sara had to go. "Sara has to get back to the store, and I guess I'd better go check out that land I now own. I don't know how to thank you or pay you back, but I promise that if you ever need anything from me or my family, you've got it." He hugged Deidre. "Ben's right. You are an angel sent from God. God bless you, Deidre."

CHAPTER 20

It was a beautiful day for a wedding. Deidre was glad there wasn't a cloud in the sky, and the temperature was picture-perfect. Thank goodness the wedding was being held outdoors. It had been close to a year since Deidre had been back to Ben's house. Now it was the Matthews' brand-new home. Carissa and Daniel asked Sara and John if they could hold their wedding in the new flower garden, which now had a gazebo. Sara was thrilled and worked constantly all summer to make it as perfect as possible. Carissa told Deidre that Sara had added a lot of decorative pots with flowers in the garden and on the porch.

During the ride to the wedding, Deidre and Brad talked about everything that had happened since Deidre and the girls had first met Ben. Some were happy memories, and others were still hard to think about.

For the first time, Brad shared his thoughts about why she and the girls had met Ben. "I'm not sure that it was Ben who came into your life. I think it was Annie that became a big part of your life." Deidre wasn't quite sure what Brad was talking about. "When you were in the hospital, Ben talked about Annie and you and how much the two of you were alike. Both of you are good and godly women, and you both always thought about the other person before yourselves. I think Annie sent you to Ben at a time when he had given up on life. I think she took care of him through all of you, and I think she continued to love him through you guys. Annie was there all the time. Think about it, Deidre. You said even though you had never met Annie, you felt like you knew her. Well, I think Annie's spirit became one with your spirit. Some people call it an angel. Others call it a spiritual guide. I call it Annie's spirit."

Deidre was so intrigued by what Brad was saying that once he stopped speaking, she didn't know quite what to say. "Wow, Brad, I'm not sure, but I think that's the most profound thing I've ever heard you say. Where did all that come from?"

He smiled. "I have my moments."

Deidre's cell phone rang then. When she looked at who was calling, she had to chuckle. "It's our bride calling."

When she answered, Carissa was jabbering a mile a minute. Deidre waited for her to stop. For a minute she didn't think that was going to happen. "Now if you want to say all that again but ten times slower, we might get somewhere with this conversation."

"I was wondering where you are because I wanted you to take a lot of pictures before the wedding. I thought you would have been here an hour ago. Did Grandpa pick up the chairs from the church? I hope so because if he forgot, we're really going to be short on chairs. And please tell me you remembered the box with the jewelry from the attic?"

Deidre put her on speaker phone so that Brad could hear her. Brad and Deidre snickered the whole time Carissa was talking. "Did you hear me, Grandma? Are you there? Answer me, Grandma."

Deidre made sure her voice was serious when she answered her. She didn't want to upset her more than she already was. "I would answer if you'd give me half a chance. Yes, we remembered everything, and we will be there in about ten minutes. We just got off the interstate. Now please calm down, or you're not going to be able to enjoy this perfect day."

Carissa calmed down for a moment. "I know, Grandma. It's just I'm so nervous. I'll be much better when you get here. Please hurry." Carissa hung up without even saying good-bye.

Deidre wasn't sure that they turned on the right road from the street. Brad stopped for a minute. Brad looked around. "Wow, this is all totally different. They got rid of a lot of trees, and look at this road. It looks like he's blacktopped it from the street all the way to the house."

As they were driving toward the house, they looked at the woods and saw that a lot of trees and brush had been cleared away. They came to the path that led to Ben and Annie's place. "Oh, look. John cleared a lot of stuff away from there too, and he's put rock down. I can't wait to see it later."

Finally they arrived to the clearing where the garden and house were. They both were in complete shock. The first thing they saw was the house.

John and Sara had built the house to resemble the one that Ben and Annie had lived in. It was a lot newer, but it looked just like it. The garden was no longer right in front of the house. It was more to the side, but there was still some in the front area. They placed the new gazebo to the left of the house. Brad pointed out where the shack used to be. It still had the look of a shack, but it was bigger now. It was a garage just like the old shack.

They continued to look at everything as they got out of the car. John and Sara both came out of the house to greet them. Sara had her hair cut and fixed for the wedding. The dress she wore flattered her figure. She looked so much younger. John had a dark tan and looked like he was a foot taller by the proud way he held himself. They were greeting each other when André came out of the house and walked up to her grandmother and took her by the arm. "Hi, Grandpa. Come on, Grandma. You've got to get in the house before Carissa drives us all crazy. I'm about to dunk her head in the toilet to cool her off." They all laughed, and Sara agreed that Carissa was very nervous.

André went ahead of them back into the house as Sara took Deidre by the arm and walk together up on the porch and into the house. Deidre didn't care how frantic Carissa was. She had to stop and look at the new house. The outside might have looked the same as the old house, but the inside was totally different. "Oh, Sara, this is breathtaking." The living room was large and bright. You could see through to the kitchen, and Sara showed her the family room in the back next to the kitchen. They had made the house larger in the back, and there was a screened-in room from the family room. You could see the creek perfectly, and the land on the other side of the creek that had once belonged to Deidre was now a bean field. The kitchen was large, and it opened to the family room.

Deidre looked at Sara. "It's all so perfect. Oh, Sara, I'm so happy for you and John."

She hugged Sara and then heard André yelling, "Grandma, please, please hurry. You can look at everything later."

Sara walked Deidre over to the stairs. "We can talk later." Deidre agreed and went up the stairs.

The upstairs wasn't anything like the old house either. She stopped at the top of the stairs to look around but not for long. André stuck her head out from a room. "This way, Grandma. She's in here."

When she stepped into the room, she saw her precious granddaughter standing in front of a full-length mirror with Beth, her mother, standing next to her. Beth smiled at Deidre. "Well, Grandma, what do you think of our girl?"

Deidre handed her camera over to André and handed the box with the jewelry in it to Beth. She stepped up to Carissa and gently put her hands on each of Carissa's hands and spread them out like an angel's wings. "She's breathtaking like an angel. You couldn't look more beautiful."

André commented, "Except for when she puts that jewelry on."

Deidre disagreed, "That jewelry won't add a bit of beauty to her, just some glitter."

Carissa's smiling face turned serious. "Are you saying I shouldn't wear the jewelry?"

André commented, "Oh no! Here she goes again."

Deidre calmly assured her that wasn't what she meant. Beth asked what Deidre thought about the dress. Deidre looked at André and then Carissa. "I'm glad you took your cousin's advice and had this dress altered and changed to what you like. Just think. This dress was worn here once before many, many years ago."

Beth held the box while Deidre opened it and brought out the necklace. "Beth, why don't you hand the box to André and put the necklace on Carissa. I'll take the pictures." Deidre took pictures of Beth putting the necklace, earrings, and bracelet on her daughter. They decided not to use the ring. Then they took some traditional pictures of the mother putting the veil on, and they got some shots of mother and daughter and then Carissa with André as her maid of honor. André took pictures of Deidre and Carissa and then Deidre, Beth, and Carissa together. André made sure the path was clear so that they could take pictures of Carissa outside in the back and at the gazebo. Then André asked Sara if she could take a picture of the four of them. After all those pictures were done, it was time for Deidre to move on to Daniel and his best man and parents.

Brad walked up to her while she was taking pictures. "Are you going to be able to take all the pictures you need to take and still enjoy the wedding and reception?"

Deidre thought about that once, but Carissa insisted that her grandmother be her wedding photographer. "Between me and André,

I think we'll be able to cover it. Besides, your granddaughter is very persuasive."

A voice behind her added, "You mean she's a spoiled brat that gets her way all the time?"

Deidre turned around to Taylor, her son and Carissa's father. "I think that's what I said but in a different way."

"I heard you were looking for me so that you could take some pictures of Carissa and me. No one let me see her until picture time so that you could get my expression or something like that. Did you get your picture taken with her yet, Dad?"

Brad shook his head no, and Deidre told both of them they were going now to see her.

When Deidre took pictures of other people's weddings, she always loved the way the father looked at his daughter for the first time in her wedding dress. This time it was her son looking at his daughter, and it brought tears to Deidre's eyes.

It was a small wedding with about ninety to one hundred in attendance. The chairs were placed just before the flower garden, and there was a path from the chairs to the gazebo that was lined with sizeable rocks. The gazebo was beautifully decorated with tulle and white paper bells along with green vineries with small white flowers in them. André was the only one standing up with Carissa, and Daniel only had his best friend standing next to him as his best man. Deidre did her normal professional work, but she found that it was a lot more difficult because she kept getting so emotional. She would find herself staring at the both of them before she realized she needed to take pictures.

The wedding went off without a single hitch, and the reception was held behind the house. They had put up a large white tent for the reception since a lot of the trees were gone after the fire. Once again everything was perfectly planned. They decorated the tent with wedding decorations and had a beautiful table set up for the wedding party. After all the traditional post-wedding pictures were done out front, they moved to the back to join everyone else for the reception. Soon after the traditional reception ceremony, they removed a lot of the tables to make room for the dancing. Deidre's grandson Ryan had brought a large music system that also had a karaoke system.

Deidre was very proud of how Carissa and Daniel kept the wedding expenses down to a reasonable price. She had taken pictures of weddings that had cost thousands of dollars. Parents would go in deep debt just for a wedding. She always loved the smaller, quainter weddings like this one. Deidre was glad André helped her by taking some of the pictures. André had also brought about ten disposable cameras so that people could take pictures of things going on to give to the bride and groom later. A member of the Matthews family took home movies of the wedding and receptions. So everything was covered, and it wasn't going to cost them a dime.

Daniel and Carissa walked hand in hand up to Deidre and Brad. "Grandma, we have a special request of a picture we would like to have you take."

Deidre looked over to where André was taking pictures. "Okay, but André has my camera, so if you want, she can take it for you."

Carissa looked at André and then at Daniel. Then Daniel spoke for her. "We know André would do a perfect job, but for sentimental reasons we'd like for you to take them."

Deidre didn't ask why. She was used to having special requests, some of which often seemed very strange. She walked up to André to get her camera and told her there was a special request. André wasn't a bit offended "Can I come along? I love special request pictures. A lot of the times, they're really different if you know what I mean."

When they returned, there was a group of family members standing with Daniel and Carissa. Carissa explained, "They're all going with us. We're going out to Ben and Annie's place. We'd like to include them in our wedding since they're the ones who brought us together." Deidre liked the way Carissa said Ben and Annie's place. As they were walking toward the trail, Carissa stepped next to Deidre. "You're really going to be surprised at how nice John has made the grave site."

The trail was so much nicer and easier to walk on. Carissa was right. When they reached the grave site, Deidre was completely surprised. John had replaced the stones with ones that were just like the others, but now they were both new. He also replaced the cherubs on each stone, but now there was a tall, narrow monument about four feet tall that came to a point on top. It was placed in the middle between the two just behind their headstones. John had engraved "Crawford" on it, and then they outlined the two graves with rocks. It was so elegantly done.

Deidre went on and on about how nice everything was and how much she liked the monument stone in the middle. She turned to Carissa. "What kind of picture did you have in mind?"

"I don't know. I thought you could come up with something. I just want some special pictures taken."

André walked up from behind her grandmother and suggested something to her. Deidre explained what they were planning. "André is going to place you where you need to be, and we'll see if the lighting is right for the shots we're planning."

There was a large bucket over by the trees that you could tell John had been using. André turned it upside down and placed it between the two gravestones in front of the monument. Then she told Carissa to sit on it. "But it's dirty. It'll get my gown dirty." Brad took off his jacket and sat it on the bucket. Once Carissa was situated, André spread Carissa's dress out in front of her. Then they had Daniel stand just to the right of her. The lighting was perfect, and so was the setting. They took other pictures of the two of them in different poses.

Once they were done, everyone started back to the reception except for Deidre. She stayed behind. Brad thought about staying with her but decided she probably wanted to be alone for a while. "I'll meet you back at the house." Deidre thanked him.

Deidre could hear from a distance the sounds of the party. She sat down on the large rock. "Well, Ben, Annie, I don't know what to say except thank you for coming into our lives and making it all so much better. We're all so blessed to have had you in our lives, Ben. And Annie, thanks for sharing Ben with us." She stood at the foot of their graves. "May you both rest in peace together." She didn't say good-bye. She just walked away.

They all watched as Carissa threw her bouquet. Serena caught it but then handed it to André. "You need it more than I do." André hit her with the bouquet. Everyone in the crowd laughed. Then the bride and groom left to start their new life together. They were staying in a motel in Richmond that night and then heading out for their honeymoon the next day. As they were waving good-bye, Deidre looked at Sara and Beth and smiled when she saw tears in both of their eyes.

It was time to end a beautifully perfect day. Right before Brad and Deidre left, John came up to them. "Do you guys have a few minutes? I'd like to show the two of you something?" They both answered yes at the same time. John told them he'd be right back. He returned riding a golf cart that had a seat on the back. The two of them chuckled as they got on the cart.

Brad had to joke with John. "Don't tell me you have you own personal golf course."

John laughed. "Not with this farm. I wouldn't have time to play golf, but to me it's something even better." John drove on a dirt trail that led to the barn. Then from there the dirt road, he went toward the woods.

As they were riding, Deidre could see where they were headed. "Oh, Brad, you need to turn around and look at this." All the trees that had been around the silos were now all gone and the land was cleared and planted. It was the land that Deidre had sold to him and Sara.

Brad couldn't believe how big it looked. "Wow, now that's what I call a farm. Now all you need is some cows, maybe some chickens, and let's not forget some pigs."

John laughed. "I've got all that. You just didn't' see them because I put them all in the barn until after the wedding. Carissa wasn't too happy about having livestock attending her wedding." They all three laughed in agreement.

John returned them back to the house where they said their good-byes. The rest of the family stuck around to help clean up, but they told Brad and Deidre they didn't need their help, so they took them up on their offer to leave.

Deidre felt a sadness but also a completeness as they drove down the drive and onto the road. She had Brad stop the car when they reached the road. She got out of the car and took one last picture of the road that led to the house and the mailbox that said, "Matthews."

CPSIA information can be obtained at www.ICGtesting.com
Printed in the USA
LVOW07s1916230715

447236LV00003B/3/P

9 781490 899183